MICHÈLE DESBORDES

The House in the Forest

A Novel

Translated from the French by
Shaun Whiteside

faber and faber

First published in 2001
in France by Gallimard as *Le Commandement*

First published in Great Britain in 2004
by Faber and Faber Limited
3 Queen Square London WC1N 3AU

This paperback edition published in 2005

Typeset by Faber and Faber Limited
Printed in England by Bookmarque Ltd, Croydon

A CIP record for this book
is available from the British Library

ISBN 0-571-21779-6

2 4 6 8 10 9 7 5 3 1

to Jacques Desbordes

I reckon He's like everybody else around here. He's done it so long now, he can't quit.

William Faulkner

The future is fixed, my dear Mr Kappus,
it is we who are forever moving in infinite space.

Rainer Maria Rilke,
12 August 1904

She saw the snow falling, the little hillside and the trees turning white, the snowflakes quietly veiling the sky and the countryside. She stayed there standing by the window, without saying a word she watched the boy going off down the road. Later – night was falling, low and heavy, a snowy night – she went over to the table and took the pages from her apron pocket, she said it would be a kindness if someone would read them to her.

One of us went to get the schoolboy from les Vignelles. He read as night fell, we didn't know where the sky was or the earth, no one could remember ever having seen as much snow on the cliffs. He read the letters and the pages, the sheets torn from registers on which the letters were sometimes written; he read without stopping, and when the candle went out she went to get another one, she said it would be a kindness if he could read all the letters, all the papers there were in the house.

He read until late into the night. Sometimes he stopped and looked at her. With a nod of her head she told him to go on, then as soon as they were read picking up the sheets and the pages and stowing them in her apron pocket. And when he had finished she thanked him, she dipped a piece of bread in the soup in the big pot. She said he would have to take something hot before setting off again, that it was brave of him to have come in this weather.

We said nothing. We looked at her, small and frail and more worn than a twig of dry wood, in her skirts and her aprons, all the shawls wrapped around her. We thought that it was the last time that the schoolboy from les Vignelles would come to read the letters. That there would now be nothing left to read to her. She took a few steps round the table and went to sit down in the corner by the woodpile, no longer looking at anything or anyone, and later when she got up again it was to say goodnight to us, and tell us she had enough wood for her fire, that the night would be fine.

Over by the barns, when we left, we heard the dogs barking, and further off the tawny owl in the hollow tree. The road was white with snow. We walked straight ahead without turning round. We knew that she was behind her window watching, and that she would stay there until we passed the slope and she could see nothing more of us, yet more frail and yet smaller, flickering in the light of her candle. We walked in single file without a word, in the cold and the night, and all the winter there was. There had never been so much winter in these parts.

Then we told ourselves there was no need for anyone to bring her news, that there were things we had known from the start. Things we had always known, although with the passing of time we ended up forgetting them, all of us here and others like us, elsewhere in other farms and on other hillsides. There were stories that didn't end. One day they began, and then no one, really, no one saw them end.

– Part One –

One

It must have been the snow, falling gently, ceaselessly, that's what occurred to us afterwards, the snow we'd had that winter, and the boy when he had come by the sunken lane, pale and grey as the sky and the wood he emerged from, and then when he had passed the fallow land, walking straight ahead as though it were all he had ever done, walking past ponds and peat-bogs and coming to find old women in their houses on snowy evenings.

We saw him from the saplings and the felling-area in the copse, and although he was still a long way off we had recognized him and we hadn't needed to look for long, because soon he was standing there in the chink of the door, in his hood and his old woollens, his clothes from America over which he wore, rolled up around his head and his shoulders, all those woollens, those worn old fabrics that someone must have given him down at the tax office in the harbour or somewhere else in town when winter came, no, it hadn't taken long; despite the fog and the overcast sky we recognized him from the copse, and we had told ourselves it must have been because of that snow that we were having, in living memory we had never seen such snow in these parts.

That was our first thought, the snow and all that grey on the hillside; we didn't wonder why the boy was coming up the hill or why it had taken him so long, we thought about the snow that was starting up again, falling slow and thick, with that insistence, that kind of stubbornness that made you think it was never going to stop. The same slow and stubborn snow, soon lying thick on the path, the sky the same grey as the day we carried the man behind the ash trees, and that was already a whole month ago, we had hoisted him on to the cart and carried him up there and the boy had followed without a word, not a word had he uttered the whole time, the whole time when we were digging the hole and the snow was falling we'd never so much as heard the sound of his voice, and we said to ourselves that he had no voice to speak, not even to say who this man was that we were putting in the hole, this man the priest wouldn't have in his graveyard. He had no voice, might well never have had one, that's what we said to ourselves, nor anything resembling a voice, he could do nothing but shout and call across the hillsides.

He could call all right, and shout the way he shouted, while the dog barked endlessly, we had heard it from the farms and we had gone up there, up to that clearing where we never went, from where you could see the vines and the fields on the opposite bank and all the boats setting off in the wind, when you went by the ponds and the sunken lane you would catch sight of a bit of roof and the trees along the avenue, it was a shack with a porch and an avenue, and when the other one, the stranger, had built it, a good few people round here had talked about it and wondered what such a shack could be, and why it was taking him so long to build.

We'd gone as far as the copse, as far as the shack that you could see in the clearing, and when we'd pushed the door open we'd found both of them there, the man quite cold, quite stiff on his straw mattress, and sitting pressed up against him, close as he could get, the child who had been calling, who was silent now and who didn't even turn to look when we pushed the door, as though he'd been there for ever, doing nothing but sit there and watch over men dying in copses. He hadn't spoken, hadn't even replied to the questions we asked, and we didn't know who he was, or who the man was that he was watching over, we just knew that he turned his back to us and had no voice to speak, nor anything resembling a voice, anything to say a word with or give a reply to decent people when they spoke to him. He had stayed there looking at the wall straight ahead, straight ahead he had looked at the wall, no one had ever looked at a wall the way he did.

Then we said to ourselves that nothing ever ended, that there were things you never saw coming to an end. We knew nothing about anything there was to know, and we hadn't even recognized him, Gertie's son who had come back, but discovering the two of them in that gloom and all the grey of winter, that's what we had told ourselves, nothing had an end, history repeated itself, with different faces and different words, different blue skies or different bad rain, and endless autumns always, so cold, so grey that each time it was as though we were never going to see the sun again.

Not knowing anything, or thinking it was him, or recognizing him the way you recognize your own when they return; despite the passing of time and the fact that we are never really the same, any of us, nor the world around us. We didn't recognize him that evening any more than we had on other evenings, and it wasn't for want of time, no, it wasn't time, he was there quite cold, quite stiff, rolled up at our feet as though asleep, and all we did was look at him. For the sake of looking at him we looked at him.

He had come as he had gone, without saying a word or speaking to anyone, when towards the end of the winter he had begun to wander about over by the alleys and the warehouses, and further up towards the salt shed with the men the ships brought back from America, no one here had given him a thought, neither the people up at the harbour, nor we ourselves, farming the fields at the edge of town and spending the evenings with the loads we brought back on our tip-carts. It was too long since we'd seen him, too long since he'd been away.

He hadn't said a word. Not that he was back from America or that he was the son of Gertie, the old woman on the hillside. He hadn't even gone to see her up at les Lutz where she still lived.

You'd have thought that wasn't why he'd travelled all that way, the miles and miles that brought him from there to here, so that he would be recognized and we would know that he was the son of Gertie, old Gertie from les Lutz, returning after all this time, all those years spent far away, yes, to say who he was and all those things you do and say when you come back, and then people know it's you, they're happy and they kiss you, they talk about memories and all the time that's passed, and all of a sudden life seems sweeter.

He had not said a word, had not told anything of any of that, he had begun going up and down the hillside with the child, the little mulatto boy, and walking as much as he could, up there in the copse as though it were all he'd ever had to do, striding all day through the copse, from the quarries to the wood on the cliffs and even further off over by the farms, asking his way like a stranger, and asking whether there mightn't happen to be, further on, higher up in the forest, a scrap of soil, a patch of waste land that no one around here was using. Day in and day out, and more than once we might have recognized him, tall as he was with that curl that fell over his forehead, and that way he had of walking straight ahead without seeing anything or looking at anything, as though it were all he had ever done, walking straight ahead and pacing the hillsides. He was the only one who walked like that without speaking or seeing anyone. At other times when we ran into him over by the farms there was hello and good evening and that was all, and we said that with all the work she had, the old woman from les Lutz had no time to learn to talk to her boys, we said she had no need for talk to get through all her work and be one of us, we paid no more attention to her than that.

Day in, day out, with the child, the little mulatto we saw everywhere with him, and the dog, and we said they weren't from around here, we said they were from America, the returning son that we didn't recognize, and the little boy who followed him everywhere he went. Every day until he found that clearing in the copse up there. He had found something, finally he had found something, he hadn't needed instructions from anyone, hadn't needed to go up by the quarries or the gardens or turn as though to go to the farms once he was past the forest, up there no one asked anything of anyone and anyone could do as he saw fit, could put his cow to pasture or build whatever he had to build in the way of shacks or barns or hovels. He had found that scrap of sweet grass, that corner of a hillside where no one ever went, and from where on a clear day you could see the river and the boats, and down below all the sails gleaming in the dying sun, the clouds gliding inland, white lined with grey, and by then another half-season had passed, the trees were sprouting leaves and the sea wind bringing rain.

And then he started going by with his planks. When he had found the clearing, the scrap of sweet grass from where you could see the river and the boats, and sometimes at evening the sun shining on the river, he started coming and going with his planks, taking them all the way up there from the port, all the way from the mussel dock to the builders' yards where he asked them to give him wood from the boats, asking for wood from the pinewood boats, the flat-bottomed *sapines*, that they broke up after they'd carried the corn and earthenware pots down to the harbour, asking for wood from the *sapines* and loading it on to his back and the boy's back and on to the barrow pulled by the dog, and from there via the quarries and the gardens they reached the hillside, and as they climbed they would stop and put down their loads, they would push the barrow that the dog could no longer pull, or else it would be the child, the little mulatto, dropping a plank on the way and stopping, telling him not to wait.

And when we asked where they were going like that, the man mentioned a shack he was building in the copse, he spoke with that accent that people used over there, and then he turned his back and went on his way, quickening his pace as though time were pressing on him, or as though he had better things to do than stop to talk with people from these parts, he continued on as far as the clearing where he started carving the wood and assembling it, separating out the planks, the short ones from the longer ones, and the deal from the heavy oaken planks, arranging them on the ground and making something resembling a series of fish-scales that he cut out and laid on the grass, imagining one wall after another and the roof to finish it off, four sections of the same pale, smooth wooden shingles, it would grow paler with the rain and the river air, it would be polished pearly and grey, that's what he said, he talked about the houses over there all in tiles polished by the wind, the rain.

The little he did say was about that shack and the tiles he was cutting from the wood, the wooden shingles like the ones they put on the houses, the walls, the gables over there, he was never done carving and adjusting them, and we said that no one had ever taken so much time over the building of a shack, that in our opinion it would take a long time for that shack to be built, all summer and the beginning of the autumn and there was always something to be made or remade, a vertical, a wall or a section of roof.

Time passed and nothing came to an end, not the making of the shack or the coming and going with the planks up there where they carried them, you'd have wondered if his work would ever be finished, if he even planned to finish it. Because when he had got everything to the height he wanted it then put up the four sections of roof and the ridgepiece, he set about making the porch and its awning on the two columns of pale wood, saying the shack needed a porch and an avenue in front of it, that you couldn't build a house, however modest, without a porch or an avenue leading up to it, he planted the avenue, those yew trees he had found somewhere or other. When we passed by we noticed the avenue in the copse, the thirty yew trees leading up to the porch, and we wondered why, in front of what was after all nothing but a shack, he had put an avenue and a porch, never in our lives had we seen a shack like that, covered with shingles and with a porch and a tree-lined avenue, never in our lives had we seen anything of the kind.

We said what he had in mind was the houses they had over there, with their terraces and porches and their avenues of orange trees, that's what we said. And also that there was no reason why that should stop, there was no more reason for him to stop carrying his planks up there and building that shack than there had been for him to start building it in the first place. Or for him to finish it one day. And we said that once he had made up his mind to build a shack, he would spend all the time God gave him building it, and he could even, if the fancy took him, build a whole row of shacks up there in the clearing.

We ran into them over by the fallow fields with our tip-carts, or further off by the big cornfields and the acres of hemp, in the morning with their planks and in the evening when they came back, the sun passed behind the ash trees and night fell, they reached the river and the end of the harbour, the alleys at the top of the town where they disappeared in the fading day, the noises, the smells of evening.

Sometimes the boy dawdled, dragged his feet, and then they waited and looked at the ships; no shortage of boats here on the Nantes River, boats carrying wines and grains, and salt and wood from the marshes, ships setting sail for Africa with cat-skins and silver bells, blue Indian cotton, and bags of rice-flour and beans from Marennes, picking up Negroes down there, stowing them in the holds of the ships and taking them to America, plenty of ships around here, ships that travelled a long way and took months, years to come back. They watched the boats, the ones putting in to the river and the others going down to the sea, sails being furled and paid out again, then back they went, up the alleys to the top of the town, the old parts where no doubt they were lodged in return for a bit of work and some services rendered, a garret, a loft in a back yard somewhere, or one of the attic rooms above the shops. Every day we saw them passing by, and in the end we paid no more attention to them than that. Not to the man nor to the planks he was forever carrying up there. Nor to the boy who followed him in silence. With our strips of land and the worry they gave us and the hemp field that gave us work for the evening, we had hardly any time for anything else, we had never had that, certainly not to meddle in matters that were no concern of ours.

Then one evening when the man doesn't come back down we barely notice. One day at the start of the rains he stays up there, we don't see him

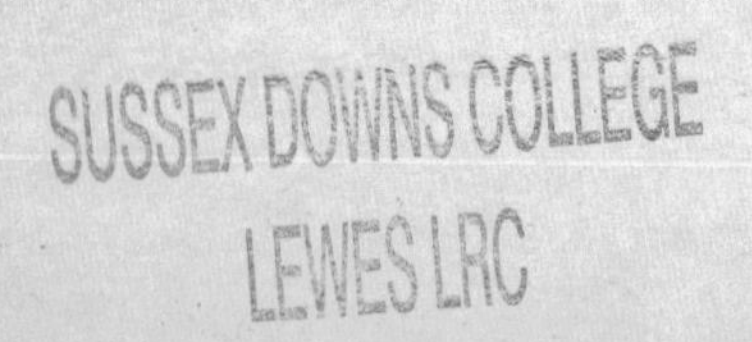

coming down either that night or later on when the winter really sets in. And when in the days that follow the boy begins going up and down with his baskets, we aren't any more surprised than we were before, we say that they've finished with the shack and all their planks and that way of going on that we don't much understand. For a while we pay no attention to anything, not to the man we no longer see, or to the child, the little mulatto who spends the afternoon with his baskets, and comes down in the evening on the stroke of five. An hour to get there, an hour to come back, from the port to the quarries, and from there via the rabbit-warrens to the clearing, and it starts raining, a little rain from the coast, heavy, bright above the roofs, above the river where it patters gently, he slips his way among the sacks and rigging, the red and brown sails and the carts on the cobbles, not even seeking shelter or, like the others, watching the ships entering the river, the big ships with all their sails in the wind, and the scows and lighters coming and going from the sea.

Yes all through the rains he brings his baskets up there. Later we remember the fogs and rains that start around noon and last the rest of the day, God knows it rains that season, it rains until the river has swollen with all its waters and reached the meadow on the other side, leaving dead animals in the pastures and scrub on the banks, and sometimes the sun appears again, lighting the meadows and the vines, for a moment the sky turns blue with big white clouds lined with grey gliding inland, towards Montluc and further off towards Ancenis, and at the bottom right against the horizon, the strip of green that you see in the spring between showers.

It never stops raining. Autumn and the end of autumn, and December right through to Christmas, until the winter and the cold come, and the boy has nothing left to bring up, not soup or boiled meat or anything else.

And then we hear what we hear, the dog barking and the boy calling and crying across the hillside, running and stumbling in the clearing, we heard it from the farms, and we go up there in the grey and the cold and the whole of that evening as it falls. And when we reach the edge of the wood we saw him going back to the shack, he isn't running now, he is walking down the avenue with the dog as the rain start up again and the wind up by Miseri, and when we go in we find them side by side, the man cold and stiff on his straw mattress, and pressed against him motionless and silent and not even turning his head when we push open the door, the little mulatto boy watching over him without moving or saying a word, not answering when we speak to him, as though it were all he'd ever done, watching over dying people without saying a word or seeing a soul, while the rain starts up, the cold and the wind from inland, not even turning to see us coming, as though he hadn't been calling, as though he hadn't been yelling himself hoarse for us to come, calling across the hillside, grey in the grey day, silent and resigned as animals or people with nothing left to hope for, suddenly ignoring us, forgetting us along with his calls and his cries and all his fear in the clearing in the wood, clothed in grey, the drab, dirty grey of old linen washed too many times; his shoulders trembled, they moved gently, we see his frail back and neck and the light on his skin, daylight falling on his brown skin, his skin slowly darkening.

We said it's a shame and all those things you think and say at such times, we think he will finally talk, move and say he is cold and he is hungry, and we stand there waiting, we stay silent too, in the cold, the gloom. In the little light that there was we see the gleam of the wooden shingles from the *sapines*, designed and then carved from the wood all those shingles in the shape of fish-scales that formed the walls. And on the ground some shavings that lie there, pale, almost gleaming on the beaten earth from which every so often an insect with a bluish-black shell, spared by the cold, by the winter, emerges and walked back and forth across the floor of the shack. And later when we talk of bringing him down and taking him with us, he shakes his head, puny and thin, with those eyes that fill the whole of his face, those two bright pools against his brown skin, about seven or eight years old, hardly more than that. You would wonder if that wasn't what he wanted, if he didn't want to have done with this winter and this country at the end of the world that he'd been brought to. His shoulders tremble, moving gently, we saw his shoulders trembling and his knees, he lowers his head and looked at his hands, his trembling legs, or the wall in front of him, he looks at it for so long that we tell ourselves that it isn't the wall he is looking at but the part of the forest and the clearing behind the wall, and further off the forest, the sea that brought him, despite the wall, despite the rain that is starting up again and beating down on the clearing and the little wood, perhaps he can still see the sea and far beyond the sea, many days' journey away, the island and the coffee plantations. That's what we say to ourselves, and time would doubtless have to pass, and even if it passed as it usually did it would doubtless be a while before he stopped thinking about what, eyes closed and all the walls in the world in front of him, he is thinking that evening.

Then, in order to forget, we forget, we forget the old woman's son that we found dead in the shack, we forget that it was he, the son, the last one, and that she had sent him over there. We forget, and it was not for want of looking at him, curled up at our feet on his straw mattress, that pile of fabrics painted with flowers and birds with straw and rags sticking out of it, and the boy sitting pressed up against him, as close as he could be. When we pull the door open he barely looks up to see us go, he stays there as though he isn't afraid of the night to come and the man lying stiff and cold on his straw mattress, cold and stiff as the winter that has taken him.

Everything we can forget we forget, and we still don't know who they are, but seeing both of them in that shack, the dead man and the boy sitting close to him not moving a muscle, we say to ourselves that some stories have no ending. One day they begin, and then no one, no one ever sees them come to an end. The shadows, the wind and the smells carried by the wind, everything tells us that stories are there for a long time, perhaps for ever, and if we should forget it, a gust of wind, a breeze damp with the approaching rain, will remind us that what must return returns, like winters and November mists, like everything we come with time to dread.

We say we have to go and get the men from the harbour, and tell them about the man dead in his shack.

Inland, as we are leaving, we see rain clouds and the darkening sky, as the last sounds reach us from the copse and the mist rises as it does each evening now, pale and cold, carried in pale clouds by the wind, haloed in the lights from the port through which we can hear calls and cries, the men from the drydock going home, or in the dusk a boat carrying salt and wood from the marshes, or perhaps another of those big sailing ships that have come from a long way off, with all those voices talking, all those unknown languages.

We walk without a word, some ahead and some behind, through the wood and the saplings, it's as though we never stop walking, going down to the river, sometimes one of us turns round and looks inland over a shoulder, mentions the coming rain and the cold, the rabbit-warren that will freeze.

At the quarries we make out the men at the harbour, we call out to them that there's a man dead in the copse, tomorrow we will carry him over to the other side beyond the ash trees. They look at us, and, waving their arms, they call out an answer that we can't make out; the wind is rising, taking away words and cries, carrying them to the salt sheds along with the smoke from the drydock, the smell of the birch fires on the hulls, with the last boats entering the river, heading up towards Gloriette and Petite-Hollande. Through the rain that is just beginning we can make out the men, the occasional cry or the soft glide of a sail, we think about the ships coming from far away, the men in the ships, one morning when the wind is up they will carry out their manoeuvres and go down to the sea, amidst a noise of chains, a long, dull creak, they will leave their anchorage and set off for Africa and then to America where they will bring the men from Africa, for years, centuries now they have been leaving for the island of Gorée, for Juda, where they will pick up African Negroes and take them to America.

They leave for India and for China, for one or other of the seven seas, they leave for the world, for months and years, and when they come back they aren't the same, that's what they say when they come back, that they aren't the same, and that they will never sail again, that voyages on the sea are nothing but a great misfortune. Without seeing them we know they are there, in the night, in the mist on the river, the ships and the men who call after the wind on the open sea, and in the taverns in the evening they remember the red eyes of the sea-bream and the green gold of its skin. They come back from so far away that one day they aren't the same, by the end they don't know what is going on, not the days or the nights, or the passing of time, then they tell stories that are repeated in the harbour, they and the rest of them going down the river with the wood from the mountains, in the evening in the taverns they tell those unforgettable stories in which the most ordinary things become the strangest, and the strangest the most ordinary. For as long as we can remember we have been thinking about it, some people forget their own father and mother but still remember those stories.

In fact we no longer even have to be told those stories to remember them, we just have to fall silent and watch the coming night, the deep night of fear and sleep, the interminable night of our lives. That's what we're afraid of, we're not afraid of living or dying, or even of misfortune when it comes; what we're afraid of is thinking of the stories they tell in which the most ordinary becomes the strangest, and then who can say what will become of us, who can say who we are and where we are bound?

Two

We didn't know where the boy had come from, or how he had found his way, he must have asked the people in the farms and whether by any chance the old woman from les Lutz was still around, they had pointed to the roof beyond the saplings, the smoke in the sky, and when he was past the pools she had seen him, she had said he was coming, without turning round she had said in a low voice that someone, a child, was coming via the pools and the fallow land.

And we had thought it couldn't be so, that on an evening like that when the snow was falling, and nothing in the world around you seemed to have to stop or come back to life, or when in the morning the day couldn't get going, or anything it took to make a day. Yes, those days, those evenings when things happened, when they couldn't help happening, and we said to ourselves that this was the end of waiting, of the anxiety that came from watching time pass.

When the snow had started falling she had got up on her walking-sticks and come to the window, she had spoken of the snow that was starting up again, and she had stayed there looking out as though she were waiting, as though she had never been able to do anything else but look out of her window at the snow and the grey sky and all that winter out there. She had stood there until she saw him. Until she caught sight of him coming up from the copse, in his old woollens, that heap of fabrics and rags that served as his clothes, grey as the sky, grey as the copse he emerged from.

And once he was past the fence she had said once again that it was a child from across the sea, and that he must be bringing news of the son, that was what she had said, and then he had stood before her in the light from the door, as frail and grey as the time before when we had been digging a hole in the rock, and there had been no need to wonder why he was coming, why he was standing there in silence by the door, no there had been no need to wonder, with the light behind him, the pale grey daylight; and it was the same sky and the same snow, the same sad day's ending.

He barely raised his eyes, he barely even took a

step towards her, as though he were scared to come forward or simply to move, or as though standing near the door were enough, and nothing else were necessary. Without moving or saying anything, in front of her, and she looked at him as she had never looked at anyone, then, looking at them one after another as though she had never seen them, had never looked at them, the window and the window-pane and the door he had come in by, and all of us standing around her, spending the evening chopping the wood for her and asking how she was. Leaning on her sticks and later at the table towards which she gradually made her way, without appearing to move or to shift the air around her, asking no questions, not thinking of asking anything else, looking only at him, the child, the little mulatto, as no one had ever looked at anyone, and you would have said that neither of them had ever done anything but that, he keeping close to the door without moving or saying a word and she looking at him as she was doing. There in the little house, the wooden hovel at the end of the hillside where, in the little that was left of the day a flame still glowed, rising from the embers, and when he turned to face us, bright, bright in his brown face, pale as mother-of-pearl, his eyes gleaming gently in the half-light.

We wondered how long he would stay there without moving or saying a word, and whether he had come just to stand in front of her in silence like that, just as, in the shack, he had gazed at his wall and everything behind the wall in the way of copse, oceans and savannahs, not even turning around to see us leave, staying there as though he were not afraid of anything, not of the night falling or the man lying cold and stiff on his straw mattress. Yes, just as he had up there in the shack and without moving any more than she did, without taking another step forward or even looking at her.

And it seemed as though she had not needed, never would need, anything else but for him to stand there before her, the boy she had never seen, had never even heard mentioned, we couldn't help seeing that there were days, evenings where there was no need to see or say anything, days and evenings when things happened and we understood that they were happening. We stood there without moving and looked around us, we tried to see if anything remained from before, everything the old woman still possessed was there, peaceful and orderly, all of it so familiar.

She had no need to ask him any questions, why he had come or what he was doing standing in front of her like that without moving or saying anything, or even why the snow was falling as it was falling that evening.

She needed nothing, not even for him to turn towards the window later and point to what he pointed to then, behind the house, behind the wall that place which she could see and which she had never seen, about whose very existence she knew nothing. All she knew around here was the path by the pools and the acre beyond which she had been taken one day, and at the end of the acre the hovel where she had given birth to the sons one after the other, that was what we were thinking, the lanes weren't for her, never had been, neither the ones that passed by the cliffs nor the others that led towards the sea. He pointed to the wood and in the wood the clearing that she had never seen and the shack about which she knew just as little, and she barely understood the words he was saying now, the little that he murmured, whispered, in a breath so frail and uncertain you might have thought it was going to break before it had begun, like himself, the boy the voice rose from, that voice that was barely a voice. She couldn't see or hear any of the things he said, but she knew very well why he had come, what he came to say about the copses, the clearings and the shacks in the clearings, those strange words and that murmuring voice, and about everything there was up there in the way of porches and avenues and sons dying on straw mattresses. Yes, she knew what the boy was doing as he stood in front of her in his old woollens and this pile of linen, grey as the sky, as the coming night and all this cold, she knew. She had always known. She had always known that such a time would come, when someone would come to talk to her about the last son, when they would tell her what had happened to that boy of hers.

She looked at each of us in turn, Andrès, Ange Berthomé and Petit-Jean from les Vignelles, then outside to what he was still pointing at, hand and arm outstretched, the wood and the copse that she couldn't see and that she had never seen, the shack where the son had died; and he, the child, the little mulatto, was the one who had watched over him for a whole day and a whole night, who had guarded him as you guard something that has been entrusted to you, something you care about.

The little that he said she understood, that was all she understood, that's what we said to ourselves. She understood, and then she went and sat down in the woodpile corner between table and hearth, where the shadows and the evening were settling, and the little heat that remained, she sat down there in her woodpile corner, not looking at anything or anyone, and a little more time passed, we heard the horses coming back and, as we did each evening, the tawny owl over by the barns. We didn't know how much time passed, how much time she stayed there in the woodpile corner without moving or saying a word, not looking at anything or anyone but the fire that crackled gently, and later when the door opened and banged in the wind from the little bit of courtyard where the cold rushed, the colour of sky the colour of earth it was hard to tell, the gust of wind that had for a moment been a flurry of snow.

We hear the last team of horses when it leaves the copse and further away the barking dogs, then silence, the fire gently going out. Then we reflect that she's been sitting there in silence on her woodpile for a long time, a good long time, without word of a lie more days, more years than we could count. There in the chimney corner where she sits herself down in the evening, where we say to ourselves that she's waiting. Where when he leaves, the last of the boys, she goes and sits down.

Yes, when he leaves. When she has this notion that he should go, the son, the last one. This notion that comes to her one day, we don't know how or why. She talks to him about it as though it were all she ever thought about, evening after evening and all the time it takes, as long as it takes for him to hear it and get used to it, to understand that that's what she's saying. And here in the farms everyone wonders why, and what this notion of hers might be. This notion of the son going away, and that's the notion that she's having now. This notion of the last son leaving, and going over there to look for the land they talked about.

The land they're still talking about, that's what she says, in that country there's still land that belongs to no one, land that they give you on condition that you clear it and plant it; over there, she says, all you need to do is to clear and plant for the land to belong to you one day, the plains, the hills and whole mountains.

That's what she says, evening after evening. She talks about it one evening, then another and yet another, just as she would have talked about something else, the way you talk by the fireside in the evening, the way you chat about the passing of time, persuading him, finally having persuaded him more surely than if she had ordered him to leave for that island whose heat and storms and endless earthquakes he would dread for ever.

~

And the first time it happens he's hardly aware of it. When she begins he barely suspects a thing. He turns towards her and he goes on peeling his chestnuts or carving his wood, later he looks out of the window, he sees the night rising up from the bottom of the hillsides, night taking over the sky, clear, bright above the ash trees and her little acre of land. He remembers night falling brightly above the ash trees, and his mother talking by her fire as she peels the vegetables for soup or puts on the milk to curdle.

He remembers and he talks, whole evenings of her talking about it, that kind of notion she's having now. He talks about it, in fact it's the only thing he has ever talked about, in that way he had, in a low, muffled voice, and in so few words that he had soon finished what he had to say and went back where he had come from. At evening on the way back from the field, or on fine Sundays when he came by the ponds to avoid the hillside, he would go down to the river, or else he would walk along by the sea. From the farmyards we saw him coming, we would chat. He told us how it was that she had started talking about it. The notion his mother had now. Whole evenings she would talk. That evening, then the next day and all the evenings after. And he never knew what would happen the next day, he didn't know exactly when she would start or when she would stop talking about it. She would come back from milking the cow or hoeing the vegetable garden, or back from the field where she mowed the alfalfa. He couldn't forget night falling or his mother in her skirts and her grey aprons, her old hempen shawls; she would rake the embers and heat up the soup, then, one word after another, slowly, she would start talking, she would talk about the weather, the sort of day it had been, all the things you talk about when you've finished work, when you want a bit of a rest. She would talk about one thing and then about another, and finally she would get to this notion she had, the land they had found and which they would give you as long as you cleared and planted it, with coffee, sugar cane and tobacco and all the things people planted in those countries, beneath the sun and the rain so warm and gentle that it was a joy when it came.

People were still talking about that land, that was what she said. Evening after evening and as though she knew, as though it were the only thing she knew. The men who came in search of the sea-captains and put their names down on the lists, before setting off to turn those savage islands into coffee plantations and cane-fields, those men set off, that was what she said, they took the ships and one day, after months and weeks of seeing nothing but sky and water and sometimes another ship a long way off, they spotted the islands gleaming under the sun and the green, green hills, the shores and the houses that came closer as the sails slackened, bright and pale in the morning, then the young elm trees in the squares and the big yellow churches, and still further off, along a stretch of the hills, the wind in the trees. Evening after evening as though she could see them, and so could he in his turn, the islands and the hills shining in the sun, all the plains and the hills under the blue sky, then the men jumping up and down in the rowing boats, saying, shouting, that they were in America.

Night fell, through the window he saw night falling on the hillside, and there was his mother talking, leaning over the bowl, the big pot, he saw her back, her bent neck. Or else she would come and go around the table, walking around him as he peeled his chestnuts or trimmed his wicker, her phrases unchanging as though she were uttering a prayer, a litany, or even one of those moans you have sometimes that nothing can alter, so much so that he had never known how long it had gone on for, how many evenings, how many dusks he had sat there listening. Not even when the notion had come to her, so powerfully that she could not help voicing it. That notion she came out with, evening after evening, and there they were sat opposite each other, at the table where she made his supper. Evening after evening, even when she said nothing, when she no longer needed to say anything for him to understand, she spoke, then fell silent, he watched her in her silence, and her back, her bent neck, that way she had of falling silent all of a sudden, and he said it was as though he could still hear her, all the time she was silent he heard her, all he did, he said, was hear her, the words the silences and the backs turned towards him all mixed together to form a single, interminable sentence about the land they had over there, which you cleared and then planted, after which they belonged to you and you were the masters of them, yes, the plains the hills and even the very mountains, he heard her, he never stopped hearing her, the men took the ships and set off in search of land, one day by dint of clearing and planting they owned the mountains and whole plains, when they died they left the plains and the mountains to their children, along with their big houses overlooking the sea.

Three

And whether or not it had been autumn he could never say, he had only ever remembered the grey day, the damp, heavy sky, and the sweet, intoxicating scent of grass being burned on the bank. And the woman who had watched him leaving by the fallow land and the sunken lane, who had stayed standing there for as long as she could see him.

At the crossroads he had turned round and waved one last time, and after that she had seen nothing more but, between the bushes and the thickets, paler and paler, further and further away and vaguer in the grey light, the woollen bonnet, grey or brown it was impossible to tell, like the sky between the thickets, between the trees and the autumn fields, she had stayed for a moment, she had said to herself that she would see him reappear past the roofs at the end of the road, but she hadn't seen anything and she had come back talking about the fog and the low sky, that colour down there, you could no longer tell if it was the sky or the earth, there was no way of knowing anything any more, then gently she had wept, she had said it was tiredness and maybe the sky they were having these days, it was better not to have skies like that, sometimes it was better not to have a sky at all and to be at the bottom of a hole with a lid over your head.

And when from the farms we had seen him passing with his roll of rags, we had said to ourselves that at that time of day he must have business over by the harbour, that he had found work over there, or else that he was going to take one of the boats that went upriver, that's what we had said to ourselves, that he had found work in one village or another on the river. He had set off as you set off for somewhere two or three miles away, saying nothing to anyone, barely turning round at the crossroads for one last glance, one last wave, so short and so measured that you might have thought he hadn't even turned his head or stopped to see her once more on her bit of path with her handkerchief at the end of her outstretched arm, and all her skirts billowing around her in the wind.

He had left. He had had to leave, although he

had no sea legs he had had to go off on a voyage so long that men finally forgot why they set off, why they abandoned everything and went so far away. When they didn't die of heat and fevers in the stink of the holds and between-decks, the droppings and cries of animals, the cats the pigs and the chickens driven mad by the sea, yes, when they didn't die on those ships, and if they did you threw them overboard along with the maize the barley and the stagnant water, like the girls and the women who went along on the voyage, picked up in the streets and the rooms of the hospices and who were brought aboard to keep them company, to be near to them over there on the concession land, to give them every possible pleasure and every joy and all the children they would need to have so that they could inherit their plains and mountains. The people on the ships told stories, they said they weren't setting off in search of happiness, or the sweetness of blue skies, any more than the ones passing out with exhaustion at the top of the masts, and suffering every illness when the wind abandoned them in the middle of the oceans.

In the end he leaves, he finally gets on a ship leaving for America, the *Aimable-Thérèse*, the *Superbe* or the *Tendre-Mère*, one of those ships there were on the river, where you took with you all you had in the way of possessions, your pound of bacon and your roll of rags, and then they wouldn't stop crossing the seas and waiting for the wind, he embarks on the ship and he goes away, and barely is he aboard, in the fever of the storms and soon all the heat beating down on them, than he sets about writing to her. He starts letters in which he talks of the heat, the storms and all the fevers there are on those ships, the ones who die and who are thrown into the waves in a sack with a bit of soil, he talks of the soil the sailors take with them as they take corned beef, flour and a pregnant sow, and how when the wind drops the men start praying, they all pray, to God and St Nicholas, and at five o'clock in the evening in the middle of the cries of the cattle the chickens and the pigs, they recite the litanies of all the saints. In the great oven of the hold and between-decks he writes that nothing could be worse than those voyages. He says the voyage is an ordeal, and how after days of seeing nothing but sky and sea, they see a ship passing in the distance, and they go out to the gangways and they call, and they are told that it's a ship taking Negroes to America. They look, they stay on deck, trying to spot the Negroes on the ships.

He sets off for that island whose heat he will not be able to bear any more than he could bear the voyage, those plains and those savannahs where the sun burns all it can in the way of crops, men and animals, and then he soon goes in search of shade, he will seek out shade for as long as he crosses the plains, henceforward nothing will be as it is here, when at the height of summer he used to make for the cool of the sunken lanes and you would never see him the whole day. And there will be no question of talking about it, of saying how much grief it is causing him. No good talking of blue skies and fine weather and the sea that he sees everywhere he goes and how good it is to look at, and starting to write the letters that he writes to her, no one here, no, no one will be able to say that he wanted what is happening.

He wants none of it, neither the departure nor the interminable voyage, nor, once over there, walking as he walks to find the land, he wants none of any of it, not even the land he finds, all the months and years he walks to find it, finding and then losing it, and from that moment setting off to look for it again, each time he says he is looking for it and without a doubt that's what he is doing, without a doubt he has the time to learn to walk and look for land, to climb the *mornes*, the solitary hills overlooking the vast expanse of sea and decide that up there is where he will build his house.

He walks, he covers all there is to cover of the island, in the way of *mornes* and ravines, of sun-burned plains, from north to south and from south to north again and from the sea to the border mountains. Several times in one direction and several times in the other. Until there is no longer any walking and looking to be done, or anything to clear and plant, until he has to do what he is asked, then he will do it so much and so well that it will be all he requires.

The wind subsided. As we came back up by the wood we heard the horses coming back and further off above the ponds the noisy, cumbersome flight of a flock of starlings. Night had come, all that remained were the harbour lights, yellow in the river's blackness, the deep, dense dark; impossible to tell if it was coming from the water or from the sky, the cold of December, around the torches a pale fog glowed, gently haloed, we looked at the pale fog, haloed, almost glistening around the torches and we said to ourselves that the cold was returning, that we could not remember cold like that on the river. That tomorrow the earth would be frozen, down there behind the ash trees where we would carry him. We quickened our steps and continued on towards the farms, and despite our walk, despite the hillside that we crossed on quick footsteps, the cold fell upon us, all the mist rising from the river, and when we reached the fallow land we could barely make out the sunken lane and further off the light in the old woman's house.

We passed by as we did each evening and she was waiting for us as she always did, and it was a good long time that we had been passing by andshe had been waiting for us, now that she could no longer split her wood or draw water from the well. She seemed surprised when we knocked at the door, at that time of day she used to wait, in one corner or another by the fire or by her window, looking out on to the path, and wondering whether the dogs weren't barking over by the barns, and we said we weren't the ones she was waiting for like that. We said no one had ever waited like that for us to come and draw the bucket from the well or split the wood for the morning's fire. We saw the shadow in the candle-light, against the window the vague and frail, almost imperceptible silhouette that soon moved away, edging slowly towards the fireside.

We went into the house, we talked about the cold and the man who was dead in the copse, about the shack in the clearing, and she asked which copse we meant and who the man was. And we told ourselves that she had never seen the copse or the clearing or anything there was over there, that she had never gone further than the field where she cut her alfalfa, and over by the well the patch of turnips and cabbages that we turned for her in the winter. Except in summer when the field yielded up all its grain, then she would set off down the hillside for the town, the first streets and the first market stalls, she would go in search of a piece of drapery or wool to clothe the sons or fabric for her bed-screen and when she had done that she came back, she set back off up the lane by the farms, that hamlet beyond the ponds where you never saw anyone but the people who were born and died there, the people who turned their strips of land over and over again and sowed their fields of rye, and when the time came went to bed and rested for a good long while from all their exertions.

She spoke of the wood and the clearing, and of the winters whose like no one had ever seen, coming and going from the table to the fire and from the fire to the window frame, in her skirts and her aprons and all the shawls that covered her head and her shoulders, she looked at us then turned away, all we could see was her back, the hem of her skirts against her clogs, the wool around her ankles. She spoke about the winter and people dying in shacks, she said it was a sad thing and then she fell silent, looking at us, and sometimes furtively she would finally go and sit down in the corner by the woodpile and stay there without moving or saying a word, the way old women do, seeming not even to see you.

We had told ourselves that it wasn't the sort of news to tell an old woman like her; that if you were talking about men finished off by the cold in copses there were things you shouldn't say, either to that old woman or to the others who were waiting by their fires for the days to pass. We thought about old women and the things that should not be said. We are still thinking about them when we leave again, when all that remains is the sound of our footsteps on the cold ground, the black, cold night without trees or sky, barely a shadow from our lanterns, and the dogs when they bark by the ponds. We walk in silence to the trees along the path, then we talk about the low sky and the coming snow, we say that there could well be snow tomorrow when we lay the man beneath the earth.

Yes we forget, we go on forgetting, as we pass the ponds and the dogs bark. We go to see the old woman, we bring up the bucket from the well, we chop her wood but we don't think about what we must think about. We think only about what has started over again since the world has existed, men and children in silence, walking on hillsides with their planks on their backs and walking straight ahead saying nothing and looking at nothing, and when they're done they sit down and look at the walls and all there is behind the walls. We forget what there is to forget. America where he is bound he the son the last one, and all the land there is over there. The very idea of the land, the bits of plain and hill that they give to people who clear and plant, and after all that time, when he returns to die in the copse in the wood. Very close to here, very close to where she lives, and he says nothing to anyone and no one recognizes him.

We forget all the memories and the story that is coming, because come it will, as stories do; sly and unsuspected, as all things come of which we would prefer to know nothing. Those things we are forever discovering in the sadness of our days and nights. Along with the fear and sometimes the pity that we feel for each other. For ourselves, who wanted none of what happens to us.

Four

Then she waits, and no one has the slightest idea what she is beginning to wait for. Not even she knows that, waiting as she is for the first time, having never had anything or anyone to wait for. As soon as he has gone down the hillside to get to the river she starts waiting and counting the days as she will later count the years, with that way of counting she has that helps her cope better than anyone, with her lines drawn in soot on the chimney breast or the flowers she stitches in red cotton on the bed-screen. Watching for something, she herself doesn't know what, something that has always lived and stirred gently within us, pain, fear or grief, one of those long, incessant thoughts without beginning or end, or anything that might bring a little peace. She starts waiting, she sits watching, as though by dint of waiting and watching and counting the days she can in her own way, and by means of a device known only to herself, extend time to its proper length, starting to spin, with a movement she was skilled in, that invisible bond that would, over the years, blur the moment of his leaving and the moment when he came to die in his copse. Yes watching for something, as she would have watched for the invisible, unseen and unheard, that comes without our knowing.

And it wasn't to see him reappearing at the end of the sunken lane or from behind the saplings for one of those rests, one of those respites, when by a sudden dispensation time sometimes comes to a standstill. It wasn't even for those letters that he started to write to her, then week after week and without ever failing to send one, telling her of the days he spent searching, and his walks across the country; those letters she got just as used to receiving as he did to writing them, in the evening in the habitations and the barnes where he sought shelter for the night. It was to know, to be told what had become of that son, the last of them, who had had to go so far and who worried her so, to know once and for all, and after that there would be no more need of anything, neither knowing nor waiting, let alone hoping.

For a while he talks about the blue sky and the mildness of the wind, the green, green hills. He talks for a good long time, about what seems to be agreeable about the country. But soon he's not writing about that, he no longer writes about gentle breezes that there are beside the sea, or hills of orange trees, cane-fields gleaming in the sun. Soon he is writing about the growing heat, the droughts and the Lenten heat that burns the plains and all there is in the way of men, animals and crops. About all the walking you have to do over there to find land.

For he walks, does nothing but walk. From the sea to the mountains and from the mountains to the sea, and from the northern port to the southern port, in one direction and then in another he crosses the country and when he arrives he sets off again, he says the country is bigger than you could imagine, that it takes time to walk the whole of a country like that, with its burning plains, its hills and the mountains where it rains, where it never stops raining. He walks the country, he walks as much as he can, that's what he says, he tells her what walking is like once you're on the plain, he talks about the plain and the heat there, and how you suffer from it. He talks about the heat that makes you suffer, and the rain that thunders down on the hills, about the earthquakes that sometimes shake the land. But he has not forgotten what he came in search of, he assures her of that, he assures her that he is seeking as best he can what he set off to seek, and he assures her of the devotion and respect that he has in abundance for her, and which will always be hers. He signs himself her most devoted son, Jean-Marie S.

So for the sake of walking he walks, and he isn't alone over there. There was no shortage of walkers, travelling the plains and the hills in search of concessions, of land belonging to no one. The men on the ships talked about it.

Since the time when they had brought them there, when he saw them setting off for the plains as soon as they were out of the rowing boats, asking where he would find the land that was given to people who cleared and planted. One pointed to the plains and further off behind the plains the hills with the savannahs and the high forests, the gentle hillsides, the wood belonging to no one. As they loaded up their animals they looked at the sea and the grass bending gently in the wind coming up from the sea, then after saying their thanks and without waiting a moment longer they crossed what was left of the plain before the hills. They walked from the sea to the first hills to the wooded mound, and passed along ravines with mules they had traded at the port, the dried beef and the cod that they had piled up on the pack-saddles, they walked all there was in the way of plains, seeing the cane-fields gleaming in the last light of the sun, in the wind from the sea. Sometimes they crossed other plains before the hills, people told them that there was still land over there, that if there was none left over there they need only ask the way to the mountains. When the land proved elusive they waited in the shade of a tree, they said that they had never walked so much under the sun. All of a sudden night fell, without another word they went to sleep at the foot of the trees on palm-leaves and dry grass.

They advanced like that, crossing the island from north to south and from west to east, walking and walking they didn't know for how long, far from the great heat and the burning plains, walking to the mountains and the rain that there was up there, they were told that it was the rainy season, the rain for the harvests, they walked under the rain, sacking held over their heads, until night when they looked for a corner of savannah, of dry grass for their night fire. And so far sometimes that they got lost, nothing had a name, not hills or ravines or crossroads, they said they no longer knew where they were, that they would never know. Down below they saw the sea, between the rains it glittered in the sun, they said that they could see the sea, the glitter of the blue, blue sea, and how much contentment they found in it. They said that was where they would build their house, that place where from so far from so high they saw the sea.

He walks, he can do nothing but walk, he notes that he is walking more than he has ever walked, he himself doesn't know how long he's been walking, going off and coming back, nor how many times he ends up getting lost. Everything looks the same, hills, savannah pastures for the mules and big yellow churches behind the elm trees. He records what he passes in the way of villages, ravines and crossroads, the districts that the country is divided into and in the districts the market towns where he hires himself out, mending fences or felling wood for dye or whatever they ask him to do to pay for his supper. He records the names and when nothing is named he makes a kind of drawing, he indicates on the paper where the wood begins and ends, and the position of the bridge over the ravine, and if there is no bridge the brazilwood tree or the mango tree planted by the ford. He talks of the ravines and the rain that drowns what there is to drown in the way of bridges, fords and mules that have fallen down the cliffs. We say that all he does is walk, that's what we say, and we have no idea of the time, we don't know how long he's been walking for, when we think about it we see him walking over there, we say that he's walking as though it were the only thing he knew how to do by now, or as though walking were enough, but how much walking he does no one can say, no one knows, he doesn't even know himself.

He writes letters with the names of things over there, the market towns, the mounds and the ravines that have to be crossed, and the location of the bridge over the ravine or the tree by the ford. At Croix-des-Bouquets he records the waterfalls in the river and the big palm trees, the wild cattle and the showers that hide the sky, twelve leagues from Croix-des-Bouquets at Mirebalais, and from there fourteen more to Verrettes and twenty-three to Saint-Marc, nine to Grand-Bucan, to the Morne des Orangiers, he goes to the Morne des Orangiers, then going up and down from there, four and a half leagues to the mountain ridges and another quarter league to Bon-Repos, then back to the plain towards the southern port, the dry lands where the acacias grow, he talks of the acacias and the white land, the terrain of dust and pebbles as you approach the sea, and the intensity of the breezes coming from the east, they burn the washing on the line. Of the little arid hills of l'Arcahaye, and higher up the coolness of the Matheux and the Fond-Baptiste, the cotton-fields at Saint-Marc in the tufa outcrops. He talks of Saint-Marc and the dance at the theatre, and all the people who are there during Carnival. The fine houses with divided gardens, flower beds and vegetable gardens, and the sea right at the bottom of the hills.

How much he walks no one knows, he doesn't even know himself, that's what he says. He writes, all the time he walks he writes, and not for a moment does he lose sight of the reasons for his being over there, in the evening he starts his letters in the market towns or the savannahs near the plantations, he assures her of his respect and his devotion, he tells her of all the walking he is doing and how hot it is in the country, he talks of the heat there is, and the rain as soon as you approach the mountains.

He writes letters, and they arrive, he writes as much as he looks for land, he keeps her informed, he does not neglect to keep her informed. He says that he is writing from Léogane, that he is writing from Jérémie, from the Cayes and from Jacmel by the sea. From Jean Rabel. He endlessly fills pages of the bad paper that he finds in the trading posts in the market towns, soaked by rain and damp that wash out the sentences, the words written on them, relating week after week where he is and where he is going, and the difficulty involved in looking for all that land. And by the time they arrive they are barely legible, then she says it's been raining again, all it ever does over there is rain. Unless, she says, it's the water from the ships, she says that perhaps the water from the ships, and the waves and the storms and everything inside the ship that makes things rot and spoil, it was all so far away, so long ago, yes the time it took for the letters to arrive, in bags, in the holds, the holds of the ships with their tubs full of stagnant water, and the barley or the maize fermenting away, which they would end up throwing into the sea. Letters: there's always someone around here to go and get them from the post office down below, and later on someone else to read them to her, for as long as it takes and for her to ask her questions, and when there are names to repeat them one after the other, in the order in which they are written down. And also to tell her the month and the year. She talks of months and years that she marks in lines of soot on the chimney, in red cotton on her screen.

It's when daylight comes, when there is no need to light the candle, that she sits down on the bench or in the chimney corner where she peels the vegetables for the soup and stays there listening without saying a word, while whoever else is there, from the farms or les Vignelles, standing against the square window, struggles with the washed-out pages, the pallor of drenched ink, the letters and the words that are still there, and she wants to hear again what he has just read, and asks if he wouldn't mind starting over again, she says it would be very kind of him to start over again, something that she hasn't understood, or something that she has forgotten, those winds that blow in storms over there carrying off walls and roofs, or the Sauvignon grape that they grow on the hillsides and, when the coffee fails to ripen, the barley and the oats that they sow, the turnips, the red figs. Yes, what he says about the grape and the elms on the church square, facing the sea, about the landing-stages and the churches looking on to the squares, and how that's sometimes where he sleeps at night. About the nights over there and the horses they let into the savannahs in the evening, the beetles flying around the torches.

Then the other person has to repeat the words and start reading over again as many times as necessary, and when there's nothing left to read, or when she doesn't ask for any more, she says that it's kind of him to have read for her, and that everything's probably as it should be, that he will end up finding what he went in search of. She says that's what she hopes, she hopes he'll soon find what he's looking for, it would be a great shame if he didn't, if he came back and said he hadn't found the land he's looking for. She thinks it would be a terrible shame, that's what she says, and that she's sure he will find it, he'll find it in the end.

Yes for a while she must really believe it, she must believe for a while in that land that she's sent him to look for. She talks about it all the time, and she puts that idea in his head, and then the time needed for him to go, for him to do his searching over there.

And then there are the years, the months of his walking. The time when she seems to get used to it, used to him walking and not talking about land, not saying that he's found the land he's looking for. While we are all wondering now, and don't know what to think.

We say that perhaps he won't stop, that perhaps there were some people who didn't stop, they didn't find the land and they went on, they walked day after day, we think of the stories they tell in the harbour, we think about it, we imagine the men they talk about, men like us, who get up day after day and struggle until the evening and the next day and again the next day after that they start over, saying and doing always the same things, and one day by dint of repeating the gestures the words and everything that starts over again they no longer know who they are, they don't know, and neither does anyone around them. We thought of those stories. We had heard such stories more than once, with all the sailors there were around here, crossing the seas, and the others, the boatmen who brought the wood down from the mountains, here on the river there was no shortage of stories.

But as to walking and writing as he did, we said to ourselves, it wasn't worth going so far, no, it wasn't worth the trouble. If that was the idea they had come up with, the two of them, for him to walk day after day and in the evening for him to write all the letters she was to receive, it wasn't worth taking the ship and crossing the sea. He would only have had to hire himself out in one of the market towns on the river or on the other side where the vines were, and if he wanted even further away towards the marshes, it wasn't as if there was a shortage of places to find work. He would have had as much walking as he could possibly have wanted going there and even coming back, and up there, if they both felt that way, he would have written all the letters that he had to write and that she had to receive. Yes if that had been it, there would have been no point going so far, he could have stayed here. She would have ended up talking about something else, forgetting all that business of land and concessions. He would have gone to see her on Sundays, they would have talked while drinking the eau-de-poire that she would have fetched up from the cellar, then he would have set off again with his socks, his trousers and his shirt clean and mended, she would have watched him disappearing down the sunken lane, turning around lower down and waving one last time before taking the path around the ponds, weeks would have passed, months, years, and one day no one would have talked about anyone, neither about the poor nor about the rich, nor the land in America that they gave to people who had none.

And it was probably because she waited, and because she talked about it, for we didn't know what to think about any of it. We said that perhaps he wouldn't stop, he wouldn't stop either walking or writing letters about all the walking he was doing. Like other people over there who you couldn't help seeing on the roads and the paths, who didn't stop, never stopped, one day they dropped with exhaustion on the hillsides or in the aisles of churches, or in the hospice where they had gone to drink hot wine and sleep in blankets, miles and miles from home forgetting and forgetting, fathers and mothers, voices, smells, and then no one knew a thing, not even how their story had ended. There was no one to talk about them. They were lost, they lost themselves in the endless world, in infinity, in the unfathomable sweltering heat of the savannahs and the green woods of an island where the journey from the northern to the southern port had never been, would never be, more than ten days on horseback. They got lost over there, and no one said anything about it, there was nothing anyone could say.

Just as no one could ever talk about Negroes in the holds and bunkers of the ships. Or Negroes on the coffee plantations and in the cane-fields. In the end they became one single Negro, without a name or a face. Without a history. That was how the world was.

Five

And later when the letters mentioned that hill from which you could see the sea, we thought that was an end to the waiting and all that walking he was doing, and we thought we had been wrong about the men who started walking and didn't stop, we said to ourselves that nothing was as dreadful as we thought, neither the world nor that strangeness we sometimes observe around us when we can't quite tell what we are seeing and hearing, we don't know what's going on. That was what we said to ourselves, that it was all over, and that now the two of them would have something to talk about for a while, something other than the hills that he was going up and down, the plains where the sun burned what there was to burn in the way of men, animals and harvests, and ravines where the rain and the storms began.

One day he speaks of the hill and the sea that he can see from up there, the high forest and the gently sloping savannah far from the plains and the intense heat. He writes that up there they are far away from everything, two days to the northern port and as long to the southern port, and that he would have to learn to love the rains and the December cold. But the land could be good. The surveyor had come, he had said where the land began and where it stopped, and it could be good, he had called the hill that dominated the red ravine Red Ravine Peak, and High Forest Peak the trees right at the top. The surveyor had surveyed everything there was to survey and measured the land, that is what he writes, and then he had filled in all the papers that were required, the report to the general surveyor and the report to the governor, and certified that the land surveyed from the 31st day of July until the 2nd of August 1771 belonged to no one. That to the north it stopped at the edge of widow Drouet's land, and to the south with the trees of Gué-Robert. Five hundred and fifty paces from the ravine to Gué-Robert, and to the west a verge of three hundred paces along the savannah where the mules grazed.

He wrote that the surveyor had been, he wrote that everything was going according to plan. He was going to fell the high forest and plant new wood, burn the undergrowth and keep the trees in staggered rows for the shade they would give the coffee bushes. Before Midsummer Day he would have half a dozen patches planted with coffee and potatoes, he would set tobacco plants and indigo to grow along the edge and keep the rest for the animals. He assured her that everything that could be done would be done, and that she need have no worries about his enterprise. He would write very soon, he wouldn't put off writing for very long, that was what he said. He said he would write for as long as he was on the island, that although he was working as hard as possible, he was taking the time, as he always would, to think of her who gave her benevolent support to him as she did to his beloved brothers and that he counted each day that separated them, not missing a single one.

In the market town when he bought the paper to write his letters on, he bought a notebook at the same time, and in the evening in his notebook he recorded the work he had to do to establish the coffee plantation, and how he was busying himself clearing the lands and planting them, he felled the lumber, made the glacis to dry the coffee beans, made the planks and the beams, when he set down his hoe he picked up his saw and trowel, he spoke of how they made houses over there, one room or two as well as a dining room where you slept, then later they added a gallery and buildings at right-angles to make a kind of terrace that you reached at the end of the avenues; from a distance you could see the houses and terraces from which you could survey the sea, then they made the mouldings and the drawing room, the store-room for the ground coffee and the coffee wrapped in parchment, the grinding mill, the winnowing mill, and everything else they needed. While waiting he lived on little, the vegetables from the garden and a few pigs he was raising on the edge of his land. He wrote in his notebook for a whole year. When he had filled the notebook he bought another, and for seven more years he wrote in the notebooks, he estimated that in this way he had filled fifteen notebooks. This was before the registers, the big plantation books.

Yes that business about the land, she must still believe it. She comes back from the field of alfalfa or from taking the cow to the meadow, she darns underclothes on her bench and she sees us passing, she talks to us of the news she is getting from the son, the last one, she says that the son has written a letter.

He writes about the work there is to be done and the sea that he can see from up there. The fog that drifts in the ravine and the little storms that reach them from the east between midsummer and September. He speaks of the land he is clearing and preparing, the splendour of the coffee flowers in April. She tells us the news he sends and the problems he is having clearing and preparing the land. She replies, she asks him to write more about that, and to tell her about the glacis and the mills and the coffee, all the work that has to be done over there. She asks questions and she makes her own suggestions, talks about various people, in the farms or further away where her other sons are, she talks of the weather we're having hereabouts, the winters, the summers, and how we're getting by with our strips of land, she addresses her letters to the post office in l'Arcahaye, where they take forty days and more to arrive, and another whole week to Grands-Fonds, where he comes and gets them.

She goes on believing it for a little while. We say that for a brief moment she still believes it. The letters come, keep on coming, and around here there's always someone, in the farms or further off towards les Vignelles where the weaver runs the school, to read them to her. And on the days when no one comes she waits, she takes the last letter and puts it next to the one she has just received, she looks to see if the words are the same, she stands there trying to tell, staring at the pages and sheets where the ink has run making pale marks around the words, surrounding them with pale, bluish washes in which the stalk of a letter sometimes appears, or a line in the shape of a flower, or a cloud.

They keep on arriving, even by the time he's up there in his shack she will keep on getting them, as long as there's a scrap of name or address the letters, the last ones, come, even dirtier, even more waterlogged than before, and she explains about all the rain there is in that country, or saying that the sacks must have taken water on the ship again.

She keeps on getting them until the end, unaware even of the little there is to be unaware of. Unaware until the boy is there in front of her with all his papers, and after pointing to the clearing and the shack in the clearing as he points to it, he takes the pile of sheets and pages and starts telling her in those strange words and phrases what it was that he was bringing her.

And then she had never seen so many, all the pages he drew out from beneath his clothes, and held out to her above the table, above the tablecloth on which she soon placed the candle, and she stowed them one after the other in the pocket of her apron, while behind her, beyond the wall, he was pointing to the clearing, the quarter of an acre where the son had built the shack with its porch and its columns and its avenue of trees, where every day he went up, the boy, the little mulatto, to see him with his baskets, an hour there, an hour to come back, we could just see him from the copse, and no one suspected yet that the other one, the son, was there not moving or saying anything on his straw mattress, that pile of cloths and rags that he had sent the boy to collect from the gates of the factories, over by Mabon or the Prairie au Duc and which he had immediately assembled and sewn over a barrowful of straw and dry leaves, saying that he felt the fever and exhaustions coming, and that he was going to rest for a while, and then he settled up there and hadn't moved again, except on those first days to sit beneath the porch and take a little stroll along the path, soon he no longer walked along the path or sat under the porch, he stayed on the straw mattress without moving or saying a word, barely turning to see the boy coming, you would have wondered if he could hear him, if he even watched to see him coming, when the dog would bark. He stayed pressed up against his wall as though unaware of anything, the child turning up and the dog coming and going against the door; all the boy saw when he came in was his back, the grey curls at the nape, the curls like the shavings still scattered on the ground, and all the rags he had rolled around him as though he had nothing left and nothing to do but wrap himself up in rags and hear nothing more of dogs barking and children when they came.

All of November and all of December and winter had come, while she was still receiving the letters, the last ones, in which the ink and rain had run, drowning phrases, drowning words and all the respect and devotion that he paid her until the end, he was there on his straw mattress, his painted fabrics, while she was still receiving his letters, the same as the ones she was being brought now, never sent, never stowed in the sacks of the ships, the sheets and the pages torn from the registers on the back of which he had started writing to her one day, assuring her of his respect and devotion, and the trouble he was having in getting his enterprise off the ground. He was in the shack as she was still receiving them, and no one said to themselves that he was there, that he was the son who had returned, who had built that shack with its porch and its avenue of trees. No one knew.

~

And doubtless the boy had to hand him his soup or his boiled meat and ask him to eat and drink, or even to talk to him for a moment. About everything and nothing, about the sea breeze and the rains they were having now, which were why he was late, then about the harbour and the ships entering the river, which he could have named and said where they came from, it had not been long since they had been talking about the ships, they stopped and watched the ships entering the river and tried to work out where they were coming from. Yes, doubtless he asked him again, and waited for the son to speak as he turned slowly away and lay down on his straw mattress, those fabrics gathered at the gates of the factories, red and blue with birds and flowers amidst the spirals, and now all the straw spilling out of them, the rough, dusty stubble, slipping on to that straw mattress where sometimes he still smiled, perhaps the boy still saw him smiling, apologizing one last time for his silences, his exhaustion, before turning away and falling silent once and for all, now listening only to the rain on the roof and as he listened to the rain, falling asleep, only falling asleep, his head lolling on to his shoulder, the boy saw his head lolling, the son sagging slowly on to his mattress, the bed of painted fabrics, birds of the finest reds and the finest blues, and amidst the spirals dahlias, peonies, huge blossoms.

Once again he saw his back, his nape of grey curls, he did not say a word, put the bowl on the ground, the jumble of straw and beaten earth that would soon be crossed by an insect, a stag beetle or a weevil, he saw the insect crossing the shack, the jumble of straw and beaten earth, going away then returning, its dark, gleaming shell. He said nothing and watched the man sleeping; he could barely see his chest rising, gently seeking air, breathing without a sound, without motion, nothing but motionless silence. The pale, discoloured nape where deep wrinkles had formed, as though carved into the skin, the cuts of wear and tear, marks of exhaustion, he looked at the ravaged, worn nape of his neck, and on the ground the bowl of bacon or boiled meat, and that was how the afternoons passed.

When he turned towards the door he saw the sky growing dark and the clouds drifting inland, he thought of the closing day and the sleeping man who was letting the day draw to a close without moving or turning round or eating any of the things he brought him. Sitting there for whole afternoons until the day dimmed, the sounds and smells of evening, and there was no point wondering what the child was thinking about, no point wondering, with all the memories he had already, the things that were not to be said, all those things he only thought about, his eyes closed and before him all the walls of the world and further off behind the walls countless clearings and seas, the moment when the son opened the registers and started keeping records, all the books in which day after day he kept records as they asked him to, and all the time it took, yes the days, the evenings when he went back up there he, the son, had to record in the books the price of the mules and horses, and the price of the oil and the wine that had come from France. All that remained of the day, then by the light of the candles that he lit one after the other, or at least while he was still being given candles and still being kept on, for whole evenings and the wind arrived on the solitary hills, blowing on the roofs and breaking the branches. Or perhaps it was still raining, it was probably still raining over there.

It isn't hard to imagine what the boy is thinking as he watches him sleeping on the straw mattress, and the man still hasn't spoken, he hasn't uttered a word that whole time. When five o'clock chimes the boy picks up his basket and says he is going, in a low voice he says he is off, leaving the bacon and the boiled meat that the man hasn't touched, leaving it there on the ground, the jumble of straw and beaten earth, he leaves the bowl and says it's time to go, that he will come back tomorrow, yes, tomorrow he will come back, he will come back as many times as he needs to, to bring the bowls of soup and gruel and take care of the man who is waiting for the cold, the real cold of winter, then he starts running, he runs to the quarries and the gardens, he runs as far as the first houses, as far as the river, and then there is no sign of him, he vanishes into the smell of the ropes, the sails and the marshlands, the noise of carts on the cobbles, the voices, calling from the ships to which the sacks and barrels are being carried, for the crossing, the long, long voyages, the flour and the pounds of bacon, the cod, the Cork butter, the ordinary wine and for the bedchambers the old Bordeaux, the cow and its calf, the pregnant sow, all those things like the iron nails, the barrels of made-up remedies and the batiste fabric needed for the people of the islands, and for the Negroes they are going to pick up in Africa, the rice-flour and the Marennes beans, and for the kings who hand over the Negroes all the trinkets, the cat-skins and the little silver bells that you find around the place, as well as the gauze and the satin and the beaver shoes, the scarlet flags and the blue, the horn combs and the wooden ones, the wigs, the spectacles, the bergamot.

He runs along the quays, the stores and warehouses that smell of tobacco and coffee, along the fronts of the big houses with their windows and balconies overlooking the river, and in the stone above the doors all the gods of the sea and the wind, the houses of the people who own the ships, who at this time of day are talking with the captains and the traders, and soon, dressed in suits and silk stockings, will go to the theatre, or dance and dine in other fine big houses with balconies overlooking the river, and in the stone above the doors all the gods of sea and wind.

Six

And we told ourselves that it must have been on an evening like this one when the snow was falling. Or a morning when the day could not quite rouse itself or muster what it took to be a day. Only when nothing could be seen of earth or sky, impossible to tell where one began and the other ended. We thought about the summer and the blue sky, all the blue skies, the warm winds, we thought about them as we never had before, while there before her in the fading day the boy held out the papers and pointed once more towards the copse and the shack, as though that were all he had ever done, turning towards windows and pointing to copses and shacks, just as when he was over there he looked at his wall and behind the wall at all the things of which you did not, could not speak, so all you did was point, hand and arm outstretched; just as he was pointing now to the clearing and the shack in the clearing, and with them all clearings and all shacks with their avenues their porches and columns, and then all the men who stood there one day and waited, could do nothing but wait. Yes all that there was over there in the way of shadow and cold, of day forever fading. Saying that there, vast and unforgettable, was what he came to speak of, having come purposefully and from so far away, there before her, in the fading day, as though he were elsewhere, and yet not elsewhere, and so silent; and the little he said was enough as night fell, the dense, cold winter night, soon all that remained was the pale firelight, the ash still glowing, and when she bent down to push back an ember the beginning of a flame, a quick, fleeting flash in the dusk.

He pointed to the clearing where the son had laid himself down on his straw mattress, his painted fabrics, and that had lasted through the autumn and the end of autumn, and December through till Christmas, while she was still receiving his letters, those things that the son still said, still wrote, the son wrote as he had promised he would, he did not forget his promise to keep her informed. He informed her of the state of his health, which was good, or the fevers he suffered from, and asked her to be sure to reply by any means she could find.

There had been an earthquake in the Grands-Fonds, he wrote that there had been an earthquake over by the Grands-Fonds, at about seven o'clock in the evening and twice the earth had opened, spewing forth water, yielding up unknown rivers while others disappeared never to be seen again. He spoke of the wind that had carried away the walls and the roof, it was another year, the wind had carried off the walls and the roof and then work had to start all over again, you had to repair what had been unmade, he spoke of what had to be done and what had to be repaired, he spoke of the wind that carried away roofs and walls and stopped you from sleeping. He spoke of the wind and the rains, and the extreme heat the moment you went down into the plain. He described the inferno of the plain, he asked her to imagine the heat and the burning sky, and how the light hurt your eyes even through your closed lids. Year after year, season after season. So much so that in the end the letters blur together, the same bad paper, the same bad ink flowing around the words, around the sentences, and in the end you no longer know, you can no longer tell the difference between the lost harvests, rains and great droughts and the animals lost in the forests, while he remained her very respectful and very devoted son, and assured her of his most loyal thoughts.

He deposits his letters at the post office of the market town where he goes in search of a hoe and a length of canvas, bean-seeds. He sees the people of the town and the ones who come from the port and the cays, the Negroes working on the roads, the mulatto women with their baskets of linen and fruits, and in the evening on their horses in the avenues of orange trees. He barely speaks of them, of the women they have over there the son says not a word, neither of the Negresses nor of the mulatto women who opened the dance in the gardens on to the sea in the evening, gold and garnets flashing at their throats, stockings and lace and fine leather mules, that was what they said, that over there the men went to the dances of the mulatto women, travelling from far away through the thickets and the savannahs dressed for the dance – cotton velvet waistcoat, canvas breeches and iron-grey jackets – falling asleep at the foot of the trees on the way home, woken by the morning, the damp earth. When they had got back they inspected the squares and the savannahs where their herds grazed, they counted sacks and barrels, the dry goods that they would exchange in the town for horseshoes and tools. Later they would send the Negroes to cut the creepers or cart the poles and wood for the shacks and the mills, to block the river to fill the well with water. They waited for the rains, they said they weren't going to come back, they looked at the sky and where the wind was coming from, the meadows drying out, the animals that were nothing but skin and bone dying on the burnt grass.

The son did not speak of the mulatto women, nor of any of the women over there. Sometimes he spoke of the ones the ships went to fetch from Africa, they worked in the coffee plantations or in the cane-fields, they went up and down the hills without a word and in the evening they returned to the cabins, wanting to hear nothing more of the sea or the ships, never looking at the sea or the ships. When they wanted to return to Africa they hanged themselves from the creepers, that was what people said, that the Negroes hanged themselves on the creepers to get back to Africa.

He writes, he goes on writing. And no one can tell how long it lasts. Not even she can do that, with her lines of soot on the chimney, and the seasons she counts out, every Christmas and every Hallowe'en and Midsummer's Day.

In the evening when she meets us near the fallow land or the field where she scythes the grass for the rabbits, she speaks of the letters he sends, which he writes on the paper he buys from the trading posts in the market towns, and later on pages torn from books and notebooks, which take weeks and months to cross the seas, to get as far as the river, leaving the ships and the rowing-boats in their grey canvas sacks, the sacks marked with black ink, bringing news from the colony, the crops and the wars that are starting over there, the price of coffee and the price of a barrel of indigo or brazilwood. And by the time they arrive it is days and days since they set off and no one is capable of counting either the time it took for them to arrive or the time to write them or in the end the time it takes her to listen to them as she had to every time the necessity arose.

He keeps on writing, even the letters that he doesn't send, keeping them in his pouch and later in his bed-frame, year after year, season after season, assuring her that he is putting everything required of him into this undertaking and has no doubts that one day it will all be as worthwhile as anyone might have hoped, he thanks her very sincerely and begs him to see him as her very loving and devoted son Jean-Marie S.

Yes he wrote letters and more than she received, even more than he put in the sack in the ships or at the post offices of the market towns, and when she had them read to her no one could have told that they were not the same letters as the others that he had sent, the letters that were read to her every time they arrived, no, no one could have told the difference, all together they made only one great letter in which for twenty years the ink and the rain had run together and in which he talked to her tirelessly of storms, of the heat and rain that furrowed the hillsides, as though over time, save for the respect and devotion that he always took the trouble to mention, he was capable of talking to her only of those things, and nothing else existed, nor had ever existed. And we could have understood that that was not what he was talking about, it was not about that. We could have understood even then.

And when he came to speak of the land that was becoming exhausted and the endless difficulties he was facing, she did not think it correct to ask any further questions, and no one could have told what she was thinking, not even he when she had us write her reply. From that day onwards nothing surprises her, she is never surprised about anything. One year there are storms, another year there is war or the price of coffee plummets to nothing, and the barrel of indigo that can't be sold, nothing that is sold and harvested over there can be sold, then the ships don't even bother to go there. Not to mention the earthquakes that bury what there is to bury in the way of rivers and houses, of whites, Negroes and animals, the same animals that fall into the ravines or from the tops of the cliffs, or get lost in the forests and you never find them again.

It was possible, he said, that he had bungled his chance, as the difficulties that he was encountering would have suggested, more difficulties, to tell the truth, than he could sort out or even explain, but he assured her that everything that needed to be done had been done. In fact as things stood the land was being used up, and he had no new woods left to fell, that was what he said, and the seasons, winter and Lent, and then winter and Lent again, and the earth itself, gave no one any rest. So all he could do was wait and pray to God as he was doing. He had to hope that she would be fair enough towards him not to treat him too harshly, and thanked her for the interest that she continued to take in his affairs. He remained her very devoted son, Jean-Marie S.

Seven

No, there's no way of telling how much time passes between the moment when he takes on the coffee plantation and the moment when he loses his land.

Because lose the land he does, he makes it over, and for less than anyone would have imagined, to the people who come from the plains in search of land in the hills. To the very summit of the *mornes* and beyond them, as far as the border mountains. Garden by garden he gives up his land, he writes that the bad turn of events means that at present he cannot keep the land, but that he will find other land, further up in the highlands there must still be some savannahs to work and plant, that's what he says, and she has no cause to be concerned about him, looking for land is something he knows about, he knows a great deal about that.

He sets off walking again, walking as best he can. Because barely has he come back down from the hills than he suffers from the heat of the plain, from the light, the brilliance of the burning plain, the cane-fields in the sun, and you would wonder if he really is looking this time, if indeed he has ever looked at all. All he seems to want to do is to walk straight ahead, as though one day at the end of the road he had noticed that he no longer had any need to walk, that by dint of walking he would soon no longer need anything, it was enough to lie down on a hillside or in the grass of a savannah, and stop worrying about anything at all.

He walks, he starts walking again, from over by Jacmel on the south coast to Port-au-Prince in the north, and on from there to l'Arcahaye and Jean Rabel, and he climbs up the hills again and looks at the sea from up there, he says that the sight of the sea can console you for a great deal of suffering, he says it is a fine sight, he walks and he walks, and with the passing of time, the months, the seasons, we no longer know where we are with him, whether it's from the time before or the time after, he walks until he no longer knows where to go, still writing, informing her still that he no longer had the honour of telling her the news that she was waiting for, but that he was not losing sight of his wish to find some other land some day. Still writing, playing down the fact that he was leaving, talking of his hard life and the walking he was doing again, remaining as ever her very loving and very devoted son, yes, always that. Life and the world around them were so hard that he could barely remember the days before, he could barely do that, or even whether such a time had ever been, but he was thinking about her as he had always done, and he remained the most faithful, the most devoted of sons.

He writes a few more letters of that kind, then for a long time sends no further news of himself, which means that we ourselves are left to judge and measure the passing of time. He must be walking and walking, and doing nothing but walking straight ahead with that way he has of walking.

Although there was nothing surprising about him going back up there, coming back down, having to come down, like an animal following its own tracks, roaming no doubt, wandering up there, we don't know for how long, like a criminal and sleeping by fences. When he started writing again it was to talk about the land he was returning to and the work he was being given. He hoped she would understand, and asked her to receive what he told her of his condition as the language of devotion.

~

And without a doubt she knew that those letters were the last. Unlike before, she barely asked to have a word, a phrase repeated, as though she no longer had anything to say, as though nothing could surprise her now. When he started talking about the books, she seemed not to register that this was something unexpected, or that it ran contrary to her idea of what was going on; and she expressed no hint of surprise, everything went on, that was what she seemed to be saying, everything went on and continued on its way.

If one day after looking for the land as he did then finding it and losing it on that February day when, for less than nothing, unable to wait any longer, he put his name at the bottom of the sheet that was held out to him, to all appearances quite content, relieved that the affair came down to so little, and when that was done heading back up there like an animal to its lair, it must all have seemed alike to her, keeping to the same long, arid sequence of days, that ordinary torment to which they both – he and she – appeared to have become accustomed. As though after everything that had taken so many years, he now no longer had, would no longer have anything else to do but what he was asked to do up there: keep the accounts and all those books they gave him. And then he began to keep the records, just as he had begun one day to walk across the island, with that submissiveness he had, that sort of calm acquiescence in what was to come, no longer seeing and hearing anything but what there was to see and hear, and if he had had his eyes closed none of it would have been any different. Yes, she knew that, she couldn't help knowing that.

Although it took us all that time to understand, we only felt a little more of that astonishment, a little more of that anxiety that sometimes troubles us now. Those things that happen and which overwhelm you, those things you then say you've known all along. That he died in his shack and that we carried him down there behind the ash trees, that there was a whole month of rain and cold after that, and the greyness that saps the spirit, before the boy came to find her; and that, standing there before her in the little house penetrated by the little remaining daylight, the damp and silent whiteness that engulfed roofs and roads and even the noise from the farms, he drew out from beneath his heap of clothes all those pages and papers, those bundles of pages on which the ink had run, brown and grey, so pale that hardly anything on them was legible, and handed them to her, and she took them without a word and stowed them in the pocket of her apron, yes we had to wait for that moment before we understood what remained to be understood, in the dying light. All through that winter there was never anything but a little more sadness, a little more of that dismay, that greyness that sapped the spirit and all you needed to get through the winter, that was all there ever was, and no reason for us even to be surprised.

What he came to say we understood, and we understood that she knew it too, and had known for a long time, had known for ever. The knowledge of those who have always known, not a day passes when they don't know, and they do what there is to do, and say what there is to say, and no one else knows anything of it, that's how the world is, they know nothing and they keep their mouths shut and they go where they are told to go. He had gone where she had sent him, so far that it would take him more than twenty years to come back, he had gone, all he did was go, to try and keep her happy, and whether he was walking or trying to work the wretched savannah that he finally found on the slope of a hill, and from where he said he could see the sea, or keeping his records in those books they gave him, there was never anything but walking now, never anything but going straight ahead in that way he had always had, as though he had launched himself off on a track, one of those interminable roads you're told to travel.

He had set off for that island that brought him nothing but suffering, and more than most he dreaded the heat and the storms and the earth-quakes. And soon each day of passing time was inscribed in a calendar of which he knew nothing. He could not have said what that time was, and came to consider it a country of whose existence he had been unaware, a land of extremes that would always be alien to him. Renouncing it as he renounced everything else, renouncing the passing of time, motionless as he sometimes was at the height of his walking when nothing around him seemed to move, not even in a single endless sway. With all his motionlessness bound towards that conclusion that was known to them both, like a tree trunk or an animal that had fallen into a a river swollen by the rains and the violently rising floods; carried off by the current, with nothing to cling to, no grass or roots, nothing that could stop time, the terrible course of things.

Yes what there was to know she knew, had always known. Of the rivers and of the ones the rivers carried away with them. From the day he sets off to the day he comes back and she doesn't even discover that he is building that shack in the copse, that place so close where he lays down his straw mattress and waits for whatever it is he waits for. That moment when the river loses itself in the sea with its men and its animals and its pieces of wood, yes, the moment when everything is lost and goes on being lost, and nothing exists any more of what exists, nothing exists any more.

Despite our ignorance we understand; our memory tells us. There, in the fading day, the pale January evening when the boy stands before her, the woman waiting as she has never waited for anyone, with all those papers that he brings her and that she places one after the other in her apron, the bundles of pages and sheets in which each space has been filled right up to the very margins and where in places the ink has run, drowning lines, drowning words, and those phrases that he has taken the trouble of writing up until the end, we realize that we know.

As though the whole of time were brought together in that one place, all of a sudden, and despite our astonishment. The whole of time since she brought him into the world and groaned, inconsolable at having brought him into the world, until that winter day when without coming to see her or letting her know that he has returned, he lies down on his straw mattress, and he is the one we find when we push the door open; it is he, the son, the last one and no one else, and beside him the child, the little mulatto who watches without moving or saying a word as though that were all he had ever done, watching over dying people without a movement or a word, and without remembering anything or anyone, except those things that start and have no end, we will consign him to the earth, and the next day when we return with our planks and our bits of wicker to support them the boy is still there, and it is as though there had never been a night or any passing time. He turns round and looks at us without a word, and when we load the son between the planks and heave him on to the cart, he rises to his feet and follows us behind the cart, the heavy grey horse, the heavy creak of the wheels and the slats of the cart scraping against the bushes in the copse, and while we are digging the grave he stays there without moving or speaking hooded in all his woollens, not looking at us any more than he did the day before, looking at the earth that we throw in by the spadeful, the heavy, cold and glistening earth, so heavy, cold and glistening that it is fit for nothing but the burial of the dead, and then the snow starts falling as it has never fallen around here before, harsh, thick on the road, the hillside that it engulfs in whiteness and silence, all those voices falling silent, that violent, deep, unfathomable silence, he lifts his eyes and he looks at the sky, the unfamiliar snow whose name he does not even know, he watches the snow falling on the heavy, glistening earth that we throw into the hole by the spadeful. And when in the end there is nothing more to be seen of the son or of the two planks he turns towards us and looks at us, for a moment we see his big, bright eyes in his little swarthy face, steeped in browns and greys, we see the big, big eyes with which he looks at us, then he sets off, he goes back down through the gardens and the quarries, we see the grey woollen hood appearing and disappearing between the trees, by the time five o'clock chimes beyond the salt shed he is nothing but a grey dot that can barely be seen in the grey light as night falls over the roofs.

No it's not that he speaks, that there before her in the evening dusk, in the dense, cold silence of the winter evening, in his old clothes, those old snow-drenched woollens from which he draws those papers one after the other, those sheets on which the ink has run, it's not that we heard the child speaking. With that voice he had, sweet and singing, that language in which every now and again we can make out a word, a kind of phrase she listened to as though she understood, as though it were all she knew, the words, the strange language he spoke, standing against the door from which he had barely moved away, motionless as a log whose colour he had absorbed, grey and brown and so cold that you could hardly make out a thing except in the darkness the pale eyes that watched without seeing a thing, and sometimes turning away, stared at the ground or the snowy sky through the window, and after that we saw nothing more except, once again, the brown and the grey, that deep, unbearable colour of winter.

It wasn't that he spoke, it didn't take many words to make her understand. There, in that hovel where they stood facing one another, the little house from where the daylight had fled and now the fire seemed no longer even to give any heat, she heard what there was to hear, and she did not need to be told; that what would inevitably come, would come the way those things you wait for come day after day without even being mentioned. Such words as were needed were there, in the pallors, the washes of drenched ink, written no one knew how many months ago or how many years, on those sheets of paper he held out, all those pages and those sheets that she took and stowed one after the other in her apron, as you stow something, as you put something where it must be put.

We in turn understood, we understood what he came to say about those men that the rivers took away and the things that had no end, the things with which one was never, ever done. Men, sons, and all the other people who did as they were told, after which they couldn't stop, they couldn't do that. We understood that, we understood that that was what he was saying, standing before her and without even taking a step forward, as he pointed to what he had to point at, behind the window, behind the wall, behind all the walls and the windows and all the snows that there were on this earth, and so close to her, so incredibly close, the clearing where her returning son had built his shack.

We understand that this is what is happening. That after looking for the land and walking as he does, the son can't bring his undertaking to an end, he can't do it. And nothing and nobody can make things otherwise, neither she who sent him over there and who always knew without being told, nor the ones he goes to see one evening in the rainy season, and who decide to keep him on.

– Part Two –

Eight

He speaks of cold and fogs, of a rainy season on the hill. There on the sheets that she is handed, which she stows one after the other in her apron pocket, he writes about the winter they have over there. About the fog that drifts across the ravine.

They see him coming back, prowling over by the fences for no one knows how long, and when they finally ask what he is doing near their fence, and if there is anything they need to talk about, he says he is in search of work and that he needs a job, he asks if there's any work around by any chance that he might be able to do. Felling wood and planting gardens, that he knew about, that's what he says, as well as writing and counting, and he had no fear of chores, no, he'd never been afraid of those.

Then they keep him on, they say they are the masters and they are going to keep him on. They see no problem in keeping on the son, who has headed back up to the highlands and doesn't know where to go, he could take care of the accounts and the books they had, they needed someone to take care of the records in their books. They showed him the books and the habitation as it was now, the gardens, the cabins and the masters' house, all the shops and the mills, they showed him all there was to show and installed him in a cabin near the stores, from which he could walk about the habitation, observe what there was to observe and prepare the accounts they needed. They asked for accounts and lists, and they asked him to record, omitting nothing, the money from the crops and the kitchen gardens, and the cost of oil and grain, the wines from Bordeaux and the wines from Saintonge, the tools, the lengths of canvas, and of course everything regarding the men in the cabins, births, deaths and illnesses. The records were important, and nothing must be forgotten, what was at stake was good order and the business that they had undertaken, that was what they said, and they drew his attention to that.

He did as they asked and he set about writing, so well that you would have thought it was all he had ever done. Seeing him come and go from one end of the estate to the other with his book and the bottle of ink on his belt visiting the mills, the glacis and the food-stores and the cabins where the Negroes lived, visiting the Negroes, the ones who were born, the ones who died and the others who were brought from Africa, everyone thought it was the only thing he had ever done. The accounts and the columns of figures and line after line everything about the habitation that required recording, the results of the harvest and what they went down to buy in the port and in the market town, the hoes, the ewes, the lengths of canvas and irons for the Negroes.

Sometimes instead of the big book he brought down a smaller notebook which he placed in the waist-bag or the belt where he carried his ink bottle, gourd and kerchief, recording in it what there was to record, and then copying it all out again. Nothing must be forgotten or left out of account about the good years and the bad and the roofs carried off by the wind, the cracked walls and the roads that needed mending, steam-rooms to be repaired and crops to be fertilized, and once they enlarged the habitation, each tree they felled and each cabin they built, each store, forge and stable, the wood, the sand and the tiles, and all the roofs, the walls and the chambers that they made, as well as the arcades around the big house and the mouldings they put on the walls, and for the farmyards and the terraces everything there was down there in the way of fig trees, tuberoses and orchids, they decorated the houses with flowers, as you arrived you saw from a distance the avenues and the terraces, the big tubs on the staircases, and all the flowers at the feet of the trees.

That was what he was to record. They wanted a big, handsome residence with arcades, bedchambers and mouldings, all finished off with ochres and turquoises and exotic hardwood, mirrors, English crockery. Never had he seen such houses. Nor as many Negroes as there were in the cabins all around, nor the great coffee plantation, or all those cane-fields they had in the plain.

Then he gets used to it. He has a hard job and he is getting used to it, recording the days when they waited for rain and the days when it rained, and when it hailed the size of the hailstones and the damage they caused, the years when the hurricanes raged and the years when the earth opened up below the houses, and sometimes the next earthquake starting up as they were recovering from the last one. Recording all there was to record in the way of men and animals, mules, young bulls and mares, as well as the little donkeys to cover the mares. When he writes it is to say that he's getting used to it, and all the work he has. He forgets the land, just as he asks her to be so kind as not to think about it herself. He devotes the necessary time and care to the task. That's what the masters say, and how things should be understood at that point. For the time being everything is as it should be, it's all going as well as it possibly could.

Sometimes we have news from the men on the ships, they meet him, some years they spot him in the harbour or in one of the neighbouring towns. He talks of his masters and the books he is keeping for them, he talks about the books and the records he keeps, and says he's getting used to it and there's no need to worry about him, that's what he says. From up there he can see the sea, on Sunday with permission from the masters he walks along the avenue on the terraces and he looks at the sea, he talks about the sea that he can see from up there and the contentment he finds in it.

They say that they have met him, that he has spoken of the record-keeping and the land that he's returned to, the sea that he can see from up there. Sometimes he asks for news of the people here. He remembers and can still say their names.

It isn't that he's forgotten anything. It's something else. And they can't say what. They talk of the country, so far away, they talk about time, all the time since he set off to go over there, all those years now. But they still recognize him, they say they recognize him, that way he has of walking, as though it were not he walking but someone else. Or the way he has of looking when he speaks. Yes as though someone else were walking or speaking in his place.

At the harbour where they go to get the Negroes from Africa, he records the accounts with the captains and the traders, what is being bought and sold in the way of men, sacks and barrels, and also what must be recorded of the voyage and the duration of the voyage, two or three days with the mules and the horses to the northern port, and to the southern port, and even longer when it rains, the animals slip on the paths and encounter difficulties passing along the ravines, you have to pass along the ravines with the animals, the sacks and the barrels, when the river rages they stop at the inns and wait for the river to calm down, he records the transport and travel expenses, as well as food and drink and beds for the night, feed for the mules and the horses, bread rations for the drivers.

When they get back up there everyone is waiting, the paymaster and the Negroes from the kitchens, and the women taking the air on the verandas. They bring in the sacks, the barrels, the lengths of canvas, the calicos and the white cotton, and ask for the Negroes to be taken to the newcomers' accommodation, they issue the orders and then give the women on the verandas the boxes holding the silver goblets, the combs and gloves, the swansdown powder-puffs, the white lead, the hair grips. All of a sudden it is night. They say that over there night falls all at once, they can't get used to the night over there.

Everything seemed to be going well, there seemed to be nothing to say about those days, and if there was so much to do, more than ever before, it was because he was learning how to do the work, it was the same with every task when he was first being taught it. That was what they understood.

When the masters wanted to read the lists they called him and inspected the books, they said that they were not unhappy with his work and that he was keeping his records with the greatest care, that they had never seen anyone record with such care, and with such determination to get it right, they could see that, they said. And that if his plan was to use all the time available to keep his records, as seemed to be the case, they need not repeat anything. If that were the case, it went without saying that he should not neglect any of the other things they asked him to do, and that they expected to see him do these things as they must be done, namely visiting the cabins, the gardens and the food stores, the kitchen gardens, and whenever necessary going to the town to get tools and lengths of canvas, and irons for the men who had been brought from Africa. Which was to say that the time he spent keeping his records, and which he defined as he saw fit, must on no account be taken out of the time spent on his other tasks. That held for everyone and at all times, so it was up to him to pay attention and to ensure most particularly that it was obeyed, they attached the greatest importance to that.

Yes everything seemed to be going well, it was a matter of recording everything that had to be recorded and leaving nothing out, no harvests or recipes or expenses. Nor all those people in the cabins who were forever arriving and going away, being born or dying, and when they came from Africa how much they cost, as well as all the bread, rice and fresh meat they needed when they fell ill, and all the purges, powders and washes. Nothing could be omitted, not even when they disappeared in the savannahs and the undergrowth and all kinds of disobedience condemned by their masters, he had to record instances of disobedience and their punishment, and if they were not found, the month and the day of their disappearance and then whether it was discovered at morning or evening roll call.

He counted them in all the cabins. There was not a day when he did not count them and count them again, there was not a page without a figure or a name crossed out, and in the margin the ones he added as they arrived, sometimes they were forever arriving, and then he had to go and find names for them, otherwise they had no names and no one could call them, neither the master nor the commander nor any of the other people who issued the orders. He looked for names in almanacs and dictionaries, he recorded men and the names they had, and each time the masters baptized them and asked them to pray to God for the king and Monseigneur the Dauphin, and how on their return to the cabins those men knelt down and prayed to God as they were bidden. Valets, cooks, cook-servants, pastry-cooks, Negro midwives, Negro nurses, between nine and eleven of them in the big house and then the ones from the gardens who understood the ones who were born on the island and the others who came from Africa, sixty or seventy in the years when all was well. Yes the years when all is well, in the other years all he does is cross out the names, that's what he writes; what you see on the pages of the registers is names crossed out one after the other, and when he has finished he goes back to the cabins to check that he has not made a mistake in the accounts and the names, he comes back and counts them all over again. And then there is not enough day left to keep his records, there are days when he is never done keeping his records, he goes on recording well after the evening bell and after dinner, he records until late into the evening, and only if there is any time left over does he write a letter.

More and more rarely he begins a letter to her, and when he does his letters are shorter each time, he says his job barely leaves him time to write letters. He writes a few lines in which he assures her that he hasn't forgotten her, that he is thinking of her as he has always thought of her, and that he remains her most devoted and respectful son. And if the wind rises he talks about the wind as well, and whether it brings rain or blue skies, it blows so loud and so long that no one sleeps up there, he tells her how the wind up there keeps him from sleeping. He speaks of the wind, and of all the miseries they are having, one year it's the wind blowing a storm, another year it's an earthquake, while in the plain they are still, always, waiting for rain, they are never done waiting, and the sun burns up all the crops, men and animals that can be burned. He writes that this year again they are suffering from the heat and the dampness in the air and they cannot find sleep. It was past midsummer and they had three weeks without rain, then the rain returned with the storms, and the storms had grown more intense until September when the lightning struck a wardrobe in the commander's house. That is what he writes, and asks her not to think harshly of him if he does not have time to write letters at present, he thinks of her as he has always thought of her and remains her most devoted son. Although he writes little, he assures her of his respect and his devotion, from the first letter to the last he assures her of that.

But although she goes on having the letters read to her and goes on replying, she barely has words to speak of it, and when she is asked she says that the son has written, she has had news from him. She is still receiving news from the son, but she barely speaks of it now. Most often, in fact, she is silent, and she alone knows what she is thinking. Then when the moment comes she knows. She knows that the time has come for him. And what needs to be understood she understands, at the very least she hears him as he must be heard. Yes when the time comes she knows. She knows that the time has come.

And it is not the passing of time, taking her as it must, taking what fades each day and moving on regardless of anything we do, eyes that lose their sight and mouths that wither, closing over what they have not said and will not say, will never say. It is not the passing of time. What she knows she has known since the beginning, and since the beginning she has been waiting, and not like us looking out for the sun and the rain or the mildness of spring for our rows of oats and our big cornfields. That is not how she waits. That is not how one hopes.

Morning after morning, night after night, and did it have to take so long, when that was all she did? Waiting there in the great silence of the hillside and the days and nights, waiting as we saw her waiting? She goes on throwing water on the ashes to wash the clothes, and carries the washing to hang on the gorse-bushes, cuts the twigs for the little fires, but we say she is more worn-out now than a dead branch, and that one of these mornings we will find her on her last legs when we knock on her window. Yes, does it take so long? And what must be must be, all of a sudden we understand. Where he has been headed from the very beginning, walking straight ahead in that way that he has, and nothing and nobody seems able to stop him, he doesn't stop, he doesn't stop now.

Also when he says that he is looking at the sea from up there, and that it is unimaginable how good it is to look at, or that the Negroes are dying in such numbers that there isn't enough of the day to keep the records, it no longer surprises her, and although she sometimes asks why he talks so much about the sea and the dying Negroes, she hears what there is to hear. Yes, even when things are still as they should be she knows what is about to happen.

Then where their instructions stop and his own undertaking takes over, supposing that whatever it is, it is an undertaking of his own, no one can say. There comes a point when everything seems to be fine as everything sometimes is fine and then all of a sudden, without our knowing, grinds to a standstill never to start up again. He works as much as he can and goes running about with his books, saying it is unimaginable all there is to record, who can tell the difference? It takes a while for them to notice, watching the light in the little dwelling at night, and all the ink and candles he ends up asking for, yes it takes time, who at that point would have noticed him and been offended, did they even so much as look at him, did the masters ever notice such things?

He has to spend his nights at it, and in the morning they see the pallor and the exhaustion in him, and then once again, in the heat and humidity of the season, he ends up shivering as he shivers, and seems no longer to see or hear anything of what is being said to him, then they say things are not as they should be, no, they are certainly not that.

Nine

And then with the weather they had that season, with the rain on the hills and the endless fog, it seemed that nothing would be as it had been before.

The north wind had brought a little rain and they hadn't seen the sky for three days, then one morning the clouds had come pouring over the ravines and right down to the bottom of the tracks, engulfing thickets and savannahs in a single great fog, grey and damp and so heavy that it even muffled sounds. In the evening they could barely make out the lights of the returning carriages or the call of a muleteer from the summit of one *morne* to another, the men returning from the coffee plantations or from mowing the grass for the animals, they put their corn-cobs under the ashes, and the moment the meal was finished they went to sleep near the coals.

They didn't talk much during those days,

avoiding words and glances and keeping an eye out for what was to come, the way you wait for danger without moving, without a word, only ever talking of the weather they were having, the fogs that refused to lift, day after day engulfing hills and savannahs, they said they could no longer see the sky or the sea, they would never see them, or anything of the world around them, they said the weather presaged worse to come.

Then they had noticed the light. There, in the little dwelling near the masters' house, despite the fact that he had closed both door and shutter, despite the fog and all that grey on the hills, they had seen that the light was lit. That was how everything had begun, when they had seen the light beneath the door one night. One night and then another and yet another, and at first they had all told themselves that he had so much to do that the daylight wasn't enough, and that the masters had ordered him to do the records at night. That was what they had told themselves, and that was what everyone thought at first, that he was obeying the wishes of the masters.

But the light in the dwelling was one thing and the masters were another, and soon the masters called him in, and he set off with his book to the big house, and then no one either in the gardens or in the cabins went on thinking what they had thought, or telling themselves that the masters had ordered him to do his records by night, or ordered any of the erratic behaviour that they were witnessing now. No, no one thought those things any more.

One morning shortly after the bell had sounded, everyone saw him properly dressed and wearing shoes, a hat and a fine linen shirt, setting off by the terrace path with his notebook, walking briskly up to the big house, to the end of the avenue to the veranda where the masters were waiting, and taking the book from him they inspected what there was to inspect in the way of accounts and records, while he stood there in silence, hands and hat behind his back, waiting as they read and turned the pages, after which they put down the book and made their observations.

He was working hard and taking pains, and it was not as though the accounts were badly kept, they still had no observations to make on that; however, and despite the fact that they had given him ample warning, he was keeping his records as though he had never had anything else to do, it was inconceivable how much he recorded, for days at a time and now throughout the night as well. Yes, despite the fact that he had already recorded and counted everything that there was to record and count on the habitation or when, once night fell, there was no longer any question of doing anything with the notebooks, there, very close to them, wasting paper and candles rather than sleeping like an honest man, he persevered with his record-keeping. He was never done keeping his records. They asked where this stubbornness came from and how dare he, yes, how dare he? As though they, the masters, had never pointed anything out and had not already drawn his attention to what should be done and what should not, and the time that represented, all the ink, the paper, yes did he really have no idea, had he no idea about such matters?

That was how they had spoken on that particular morning as the day was beginning and the men were leaving the farms, and when they had returned the notebook to him they had asked if he had understood a word they had said to him, and he had replied that he had understood and he would do everything within his power to keep them content. Then he left as he had come, at the same brisk pace and without seeing or looking at anyone, he took off his shirt his hat and the shoes, then with a little notebook wedged in his belt, his gourd and his kerchief, he reached the mills and the coffee stores and set to work, visiting and counting everything there was to visit and count in the estate and writing it down as it must be written down.

And one might have thought that having said what they had to say, they had concluded the affair to the best of their ability. With the fogs they were having, which had been encircling the hills day and night and for such a long time now, everyone came to see the ordinary as the strange, and think of things that should not have been thought; that the weather presaged nothing good, and was driving people out of their minds. But when they came to notice once again what there was to be noticed, what they saw was both worrying and peculiar. Nothing had ended, neither the fog nor the eccentric behaviour that they observed, and no one up there could be unaware of what was happening, no, no one could be unaware of that any more, because in fact what they had seen and heard that morning was only the beginning.

Yes that morning and all the mornings that followed. All the time until the day he left, when he was seen with the boy and his straw mattress over his back climbing over the fence, and then another season would have passed and there would be no sign of him returning. Day after day he took his notebooks up to the big house as they called him to do, they saw him coming along the terrace path with his hat, his fine linen shirt and the shoes he had for going up to the big house, and it had been more than twenty years, walking straight ahead without looking at anyone or seeing anyone except, at the end of the avenue, the veranda where they sat; and then, turning the pages and asking questions, they would inspect his notebook. He stood there in front of them not moving or saying a word, waiting for them to finish reading and deliver their observations; you could see them and hear them in the distance, day after day, from the avenues and the mills and from the Negro cabins, and everyone watched as you watch what is coming and what must come, like men stabbing one another or succumbing to poison in the depths of a stage, or a barn burning down along with its animals, its straw and its crops, you wait for death and misery, and then you no longer know whether to think about it or to forget everything, in fact when these things happen you no longer know what there is to know, you can only wait and watch and wonder if there is anything else but such misfortune here below.

They said again what they had said over the previous few days, those sentences they had constructed about him and intended never to have to say again, their voices hammering in the words like nails as they asked him to look at them when they were speaking, his hands behind his back he looked at them and answered, in the same low, gentle, almost muffled voice. He said the previous day he had had so much work he had not been able to get to the end of his records, no he had not been able to get to the end of them, whatever the season there was always so much, if not more, to record in the way of animals, men and crops. Or else, he said, he had had to start over again. For fear of making a mistake or leaving something out he sometimes had to start his accounts all over again, and when he had done that he would copy them out once more, it had to be done for the sake of prudence, the book might get lost or be spoiled by the rain and the weather they were having. He spoke and then fell silent, looking at the ground or through the doors behind them at all the things there were on the walls, the mirrors, the pictures, and on the tables the white starched linen, the gently gleaming crockery, sometimes he even shivered, they saw shivers running down his arms and his shoulders, as though he were suffering from the cold or as though he had caught a fever, and they asked why he was shivering like that. While they turned the pages, underlining and crossing out words and whole lines, every now and again they would rise to their feet and walk around him as, lowering his eyes, he went on shivering.

They asked what that obstinacy was, that way he had of acting as though he understood nothing they were saying to him. That was it, wasn't it, they said, it was a lack of comprehension, given that he had no difficulty understanding them when they spoke, because despite the representations they made to him he was still recording even things that did not need to be recorded, he was recording more and more of those things, that was why, correcting and crossing out and adding words in the margins and lines between the lines, he was never finished, and he sometimes tore out pages, they observed that some pages had been torn out, which was hardly customary record-keeping practice, no one had ever torn pages out of books like that, strewn over his floor they could see paper torn from books, crumpled and twisted into balls that the wind blew about outside, in the avenues you could see the papers and the balls chased by the wind.

Everyone could see and hear them, the ones that the ships brought to the coffee plantations and the others who had been there for a long time, they crossed the courtyards and set off for the gardens and wondered what it was that they were seeing and hearing there. On the veranda, never taking their eyes off him, the masters, becoming impatient and tapping the ground with their feet, or drumming the wooden table-tops with their fingers and him standing before them saying that he understood, that he was quite capable of understanding what they said, but they were probably aware that you could not always do what you wanted to do, however devoted you might be you could not always do it. It was not that he wanted to cause discontent, heaven was his witness that it had never been his intention to cause any displeasure, either to them or to anyone else, he assured them of that, that was what he said, and he would endeavour to keep them happier.

So they gave him back his notebook and said that that was exactly what they wanted, and that he seemed to have returned to his senses. He set off again as he had arrived, without seeing or looking at anything, and so briskly that no one would have thought of talking to him any further or questioning him about what had just happened. His face was unchanged and he still stared into the far distance, he walked with the same brisk step, staying close to the walls and entering the cabins and the storehouses where everyone saw him bustling about and making up for lost time; yes, perhaps he was saying to himself that he was making up for lost time.

Everyone could see and hear, and observe at night that he was still keeping his records. In the cabins in the evening they talked about it, the men from Africa and the others, and the old women who made the bundles of firewood and grated the cassava. Night fell, all it did now was fall from morning till evening and from evening till morning, from behind the mountains and from behind the sea, without seeing a thing they looked at the sky where night was falling, the dark horizon where the ships came from; they made fires, they stirred the embers with a stick, the wind rose up and scattered the ashes over their clothes. Wasn't it strange, those words, those gestures, always the same, and that obstinacy he seemed unable to shake off, every day he went to see the masters and presented the register to them, while they said that it was inconceivable all the accounts he was doing, and he replied that he understood and had no intention of causing any displeasure, and had never had any such intention?

They had said that they were going to cut off his supply of candles, and that without candles he would be forced not to record as much, and indeed they had cut off his supply of candles, but at night he was seen closed in there with his light and all the bugs and beetles flying around him, and outside there were the balls of paper driven by the wind, and you would have wondered where he got hold of his candles and why he seemed now to have no fear of the masters now or their severity, although he still understood them when they spoke. It was as if he was a thousand leagues away and no longer thinking about them or about anything they said, there were days when he left the door open and everyone could see the light he made, and all the bugs and beetles flying around. Yes the son, the last one in there with his light, while outside everyone could see the candle trembling in the rising wind, and if you stood to one side you could see his shadow on the wall; to the other you couldn't.

No it wasn't the boy speaking, in that voice of his, sweet and singing, that strange language in which occasionally in a murmur, a kind of whisper, we could make out a word, a phrase, it wasn't him speaking. We could hear what there was to hear, what he was saying as he stood against the door, with his murmurs and his whispers and all those sheets of paper he gave her. That the son, the last one, had not stopped, he had not been able to stop, he could never finish the things they asked him to do, there were things you could never be done with, never finished with. Over there they had talked about a notion that he had had, the son, one of those notions that take hold of you and you can't get rid of them, as happens sometimes to a notion, it appears one day and nothing and no one can free you from it. Yes a notion that had come to him, that was what they had said, and now that he had started he wouldn't stop, even when they deprived him of ink and candles and issued all the threats and prohibitions that they could issue, he would keep his records night after night, and no one would see him in the candlelight with the bugs and the beetles flying around, and outside in the avenue blown by the wind all the pages he had torn out and crumpled into balls.

They had said he wouldn't stop, that he wouldn't be able to stop, there had been things like that which you could not be done with, it was not for want of opportunity, starting and not being able to finish, day after day repeating the gestures and the words and everything in the world that could be repeated, like puppets and marionettes, those wooden figures that you saw at fairgrounds, surely there were men who made you think of the ones you saw at fairgrounds, as though driven by invisible forces, invisible commands, and there was no way of knowing which they were, men or wooden figures, whatever way you looked at them you couldn't tell. Any more than you could tell who exactly was issuing the commands, those people never showed their faces, they were unknown people, beyond suspicion, like so many others all around in the houses and in the streets, they went their way and said hello and good evening politely and no one suspected a thing, no, no one suspected a thing. At night everyone saw the light and the bugs and the beetles flying around and wondered who on earth he was, whether he was eating and sleeping and whether he was quite like anyone, man or beast, who had ever been born and died on this earth. He went to fetch the water from the well and in the evening he lit the stove, when there was an earthquake on the island or a storm passed across it he prayed to God that it might not vanish into the sea, but had any of it meant a thing? Like those Sundays when you saw him setting off for the savannah, on Sundays they noticed him moving away from the houses and setting off for the savannah, that was what they had said, that they saw him moving off towards the savannah or further down towards the ravines. So if that was where he was going it wasn't a woman he was after. No it wasn't a woman he went to find behind the hedges and the undergrowth. If he, the son, the last of the boys, went off all alone to such distant corners it was to lie down on the ground and work it as best he could. The sweet, warm, welcoming earth that he worked with his belly, with his member hardening and digging away at whatever there was to dig. They said he was going to dig the earth, dig and hoe it as much as he could, until he fell back with a shiver and no one can tell if he's laughing or crying, no, no one can tell. That's what they say. They talk of the ones who are so alone that on Sundays, for whole afternoons, they go in search of the earth and work it as they would work a woman.

When we looked out of the window we couldn't tell where sky began and earth ended, there was nothing but grey and deep, deep silence. The boy still hadn't moved, he had barely moved away from the door with the sheets that he held out to her and which she stowed in her apron, while with his other hand he kept on pointing to the clearing, he never stopped pointing to the clearing, behind her, behind the wall in the copse in the forest that place that she couldn't see, that she had never seen, but which she looked at now as though it were there before her eyes, with the shack and the porch and the two slender columns, then behind all that, behind the wood, behind the sea further off, all the islands, the coffee plantations and the cane-fields, yes perhaps that was what she saw now, what she could not stop seeing.

The son, the last of the boys, with his hat, his fine linen shirt and his shoes of twenty years ago, and in the evening he washes his shirt and shoes for the following day's convocation, that's what she is told, what she must understand, what the boy sees, in the evening, every evening, the son washing, cleaning his clothes and his shoes for the next day when, book under his arm, he goes along to the convocation, and everyone observes him and reports that today, once again, that man has been summoned to the convocation and is going to show them the book. And although they have forbidden him time and again and confiscated his ink and his registers on Sundays, they still haven't fired him, as though this were also a habit that they were picking up in their turn, they and everyone watching, yes a habit that they all had now, all of them, as though they had become used to seeing a marionette or a wooden figure walking along their avenues, a wretched puppet who could not shake off a command that he had once been given, could not reject it as the body rejects what does not agree with it.

Yes, when the strange thing is that everything starts over again and they know, don't they get used to it, as you get used to something that agrees with you? One day when we don't expect things to happen, carried along as though by a deep tide, by seas that tirelessly beat the shores and cast up all there is to cast up, it's as though everything had existed for ever. Over time you get used to it, nothing surprises you, neither the men in the fairgrounds nor those who resemble them, and when death takes them everyone is there, in the same final gesture, the same last look. He will go on for ever recording things in a notebook, jotting word after word on pages, then he will walk out on to an avenue to bring them the notebook, and they will open the notebook and make their observations, while the others, all the others in the cabins and the alleys, all the cabins and alleys in the world, will be there watching what happens and asking why everything was forever starting over again, and if there was a word to describe such things.

All they could see now was the fog on the hill-sides and the grey of the days and nights; one morning the fog would lift and reveal the world as fixed, captured in webs, a crystal, a frost no sun could melt, and they would be fixed along with it in that same final gesture, that same last look. Yes that was how death would take them, like the bird shot down in full flight, motionless its wings open wide against the horizon.

Ten

And again if no one, not even the son himself, knew how long it had all lasted, then there was nothing out of the ordinary in that. A little more confusion and a little more distress, the erratic behaviour that keeps him going. For as long as it lasts, and as long as they give him paper and ink, and then when they've stopped doing that no one knows where or how he keeps on getting hold of it, until off he goes and starts walking again, walking as much as he can, and one day they see the two of them here with their planks and the wheelbarrow. The last pages of his records are dated, but there is nothing to indicate where or how he gets around to filling them in. Yes as long as it lasts, and the way everything begins to blur, all the months, all the weeks, the seasons. For him to stay with them and keep the records the way he does, then one day he is fired from the job, and on another, no one says how, he finds himself back on one of the ships that cross the ocean to come here with their cargo of indigo, coffee and tobacco, once again he walks straight ahead, in that way he has always done, with no apparent hesitation, no questions. Like people who have a lot to do or who, having learned a role, play it from the first day to the last, as though it were the only thing they had ever done. One day just as they gave him the books they take them back, and on that day he presents himself before them for the last time, and that is after the night when he makes his final entries.

And he must know. That morning, as he sets off down the avenue and brings them the notebook, he must know that everything has blurred into one, it has all just blurred into one, and he must know it again later as he collects his luggage from under the bedstead, his few remaining clothes, his shoes, his frock coat and his breeches. Yes all the time that has passed and the coming months and years and wandering as he does. One single great day, without rest, without sleep, an evening and a morning that never change, the scraps of intervening night that mean nothing but a little more exhaustion, a little more sadness; and later when he comes here that other long, long day of frost and rain, that road, that path on which you would think he was walking without getting anywhere, walking motionlessly one step after another, in such a hurry to get there.

He leaves, one December evening he goes back down the hills, back down all there is in the way of hills and coffee plantations, making for the plain where the sun shines, the man, the boy and the dog coming after, he boards the boat and off he goes, and the day comes when he sets about building the shack and then when that's finished the day comes when he takes the time to contemplate it, the two fine pale wood columns and the avenue leading up to them, the scrap of sky between the trees. Brief though it is that moment will exist, and then he will begin to die.

They say they are taking the books back and they are asking him to go, he sets about making his final entries, for the 29th day of December of the year 1783 he records 900 pounds of earthenware from England and 3 barrels of ordinary wine from Bordeaux, as well as the batiste, the Fougères fabric and the ell of black ribbon, and for parties the silk shoes, the muslins, the taffetas and the dancing masters, recording the merchandise and the considerable increase in prices, then, on the subject of the Negroes in the cabins, how many of them had recently been born and how many had died, and the ones who had contracted fevers from the fog.

Then when that is done he sets about writing a letter, he says he is writing a letter, the last one, he informs his mother of his situation and tells her that on that day, the 29th of December, he is preparing to leave and getting his luggage ready. He is writing, he says, the last letter from that place up in the hills that he is about to leave, he spends several days writing it, it is raining, the rain won't let up, when the rain stops he sees the houses gleaming and the terraces and all the lights, he hears voices and laughter, music playing, and in the cabins the people having a late meal of the ham the masters gave them, ordering them to laugh and sing and enjoy themselves in the correct manner. He writes that he is leaving, that he will leave as soon as the rain stops, and he writes to say how much grief it causes him and always will. That is what he writes, that they no longer need him up there, but down below he will find some work, he says there need be no doubt that he, the son, will find work in the plain, and that she need not worry on his account, she need have no worries about anything at all. The son will find work, perhaps he will even find land, perhaps there was even some land to be found in the plain, yes, perhaps there was some left. My dearest mother, as I write we are having rainstorms and, apart from the hurricanes it is the most awful weather that we have ever seen. If I try to describe my situation to you, I do it only so that you will not think it so terrible that I have tried to give everything up once again. Rest assured that I am putting everything I can into my attempt to bring this affair to the best possible conclusion. So I must now take my leave of you and draw water from the well, and see if the horses who escaped to the *morne* have been recaptured. Signed, your most devoted son.

They set off on that December evening, the two of them and the dog coming after. Over by the cabins when they leave the avenue they hear the music of a violin, a Negro playing the violin and whistling, they hear the Negro whistling and playing the violin and the music coming on the wind, the music carried to the gardens, crossing the fences, with their fresh coats of white paint, the fences that divide the savannahs – whether it is that day or later and further off, that they hear a Negro playing the violin, it seems to us as though all he does now is talk about the Negro and his violin, there in all those papers with the letters for her, the last ones he wrote, the Negro playing the violin and in the distance a woman weeping.

Yes the last letters, along with the one written from the ship and another one that he must have written in the shack, the paper is not the same and he writes in pencil. All those sheets, those bundles that are being brought to her now, to the woman who cannot read, who has never learned how, and then she holds out her hand, her arm, and takes them one after the other and stows them in her apron pocket, the bits of paper, pages torn from registers on the back of which he records, just as he used to, the savannahs and the towns they pass through, or else he starts a letter, one of the ones he still writes and no longer even takes the trouble to send. On the very sheet on which the lists and accounts were drawn up, the days and the weeks and all those seasons when they waited for the earth to open, or waited for one of those storms that engulfed towns and savannahs to reach them from the sea, on the page of a register that he has taken away with him he starts a letter, and then it's all the same as before, horses escaping on to the *morne*, Negroes dying of fevers, and the devotion and respect that he always takes the trouble to put in his letters, everything merges together and you can't tell if this is a letter that he has begun or a page of the records, there's no way of telling.

They set off, they cross the fences and go down what there is to go down in the way of tall forests, hedges and savannahs, and to the ravines below where grass and mud are rolled in the rivers; at dusk they hear the carts coming back with the creepers, the grass for the animals, they slip on the path, or perhaps an animal escapes into the wood, they hear people shouting after the animal that has escaped into the wood, they see the smoke from the fires, the blackness filling the sky. In the evening as they make their way towards the plain, towards the sea that glitters far below, crossing woods and savannahs as they travel back along the path he took before, walking to the sea they could see from up there, soon there would be only that, the sea they could see from up there, in the great heat, the sheen of the sea, the endless light of the plains leading down to it, recording the towns and the crossroads, the hills they climbed down, the names, always the same, Grands-Fonds, Limbé, Jérémie, Léogane, Port-au-Prince, if they have time they go to the King's garden to see the hibiscus flowers, the Havana cedar, that's what he writes, to listen to the sea in Jacmel, the water rolling on the cays.

He records the names, the same ones, he repeats them as he walks, only ever walking straight ahead as much as he can, walking straight ahead, and as far as the plain would take him, they pass the staging posts, the mills where they pound the indigo, they walk towards the sea and the big cane-fields, the sun returns and the blue sky. The sparkling sea.

It must be January, February, the start of the year, then a whole Lenten season of the kind they have in the plains over there, that's what he says, he says that for a whole season in the plain they suffer from the sun, every morning every evening, and that the heat is very intense. And he has no need to count the time, he has all the time he needs and more, to go down the hills and cross the plains to the sea, he walks with the boy towards the sea you can see from up there, they sleep on the savannahs. Time is one thing they have, and time to set off again along their paths in the morning, the hill-sides that smell of orange and logwood, they see the men cutting the hedges and the arbours, painting walls, fences; once past the acacias the earth turns white and dry, gleaming with pebbles, they walk on the pebbles, the dry, white earth down to the marshes, to the green of the mangroves. He talks about it. He writes it down.

Sometimes he opens the book, he says he hasn't finished, and being finished isn't really what makes a book, he keeps his records in the book, he says there are still things that need to be recorded.

He has time, always has had.

And must all the shadow and the grey and the cold of our lives return with our memories? And our stupefaction the day we are finally forced to understand? Must everything take so long? Must he go away for more than twenty years and then come back, must another whole year pass when we see him with his planks on his back, before he settles in the copse with the shack around him and doesn't come out again until we carry him to the cliff, the son we haven't recognized, while the boy still says nothing; it's only later when the snow starts up again that he comes to find her, we can't forget the snow and the boy climbing up by the sunken lane, asking the people from the farms whether by any chance his mother might still be around here, and then he is there in the chink of the door, as frail and grey as the time before. Yes, must it take so long?

Once again the son goes his way, without saying a word or asking any questions, all he does, all he has ever done, is to go his way, and nothing changes, nothing makes a difference, it never does. What she knows, what she tells herself as she waits, is that there is no difference between nothing and nothing, between being born and dying, suffering the whole day through then starting over again the next morning, always starting everything over. Or being there one winter evening no longer feeling or thinking anything, quite stiff, quite cold on a straw mattress.

Must time last so long, must she wait as she does? In the great silence of the hillside, all those days and nights, must she wait like that for what is coming, that thing to which everything has been leading from the very first, the path she has made him take and which he takes to the end, certain that there is not and will never be another?

And here is where the path comes to an end, very close to here, close to this hovel where one winter evening in his snow-drenched rags the boy comes to talk to her about the men who were carried off by the rivers, wild and violent the rivers that no one can resist. There in all the winter and all the grey, that place he points to where she has never been, where when the son returns he builds his shack, however far she sends him back he comes, and he is not two leagues away from where she is now, not two leagues from the hovel to which all these papers are being brought to her. And she has never seen so many, she takes them, standing against the table, small and frail and more worn than a dry wooden twig, one after the other she takes the papers and stows them in her apron, the papers on which he kept his records, telling of the great droughts and all the rain there is over there and the deaths of the Negroes, the days the nights when everything starts over again and the beetles the bugs that fly in the light.

The boy hasn't moved, he has barely moved away from the door, he stands there in the evening, in the dusk, and he barely speaks, he says what he knows, all that time he has seen, the son keeping his records, doing nothing now but keeping records, while the wind starts up in the trees in the highlands blowing on the roofs, breaking the branches; and the rain starting, endless, up there all it does is rain, or else another storm fills the sky and then the earth trembles, it begins to tremble. Yes the months, the years and the days when everything starts up again. All the time when that same son of hers is keeping his records, all the time he is writing in the notebooks, and in the end, the child, the boy who won't leave his side until he goes to sleep, sooner or later he does go to sleep, and the man has not spoken or said a word of the kind that people say in the evening in the houses, in the hovels, in anything with walls and a roof, a hearth to make a fire. Unless it is his turn to deal with the books, unless it is the turn of the child, the little mulatto, to copy out and copy out again everything there is in the way of lists and accounts, on Sundays or in the evening while they can hear the wind and the rain and all the branches on the roof, reading a page or two before he sleeps, and when that page is read writing out the lines, beside the son copying the pages, in long lines copying out and copying out again the great droughts the hurricanes and the earthquakes as well as the deaths of the Negroes, making all the downstrokes and the upstrokes and murmuring the phrases in a low voice, murmuring them, they hear the wind and the branches beating against the roof, the noise of branches against the roof but still he goes on copying, in long lines once more he copies out the deaths of the Negroes, murmuring, whispering over and over. He knows something about what is written in the books, he knows something about record-keeping, and in the morning when he gets up the other one, the son, is still there, and when he is told to stop he won't stop, he never stops. While there is still daylight, and then in the light of the candles that he lights one after the other, or at least while they are still giving him candles.

Now that the son has started he can't stop. He doesn't stop, he never stops, that's what she is being told now, in the murmurs, whispers and averted glances, in all that grey and cold of winter, all about him the son, the last of them, the one who left, who writes endlessly in the registers and nothing and no one can stop him, at night everyone sees the light and the bugs and the beetles flying round, and everyone watches him and wonders who he is, that's what they come to tell her in the cold of winter, in the little daylight that remains, that the son is like a puppet, one of those automata you see at fairgrounds and which can't be stopped, that there are things that you start and can't finish, like the cycle of day and night, they give him the books and he carries out their instructions, the son does as they ask, conscientious and determined to do the right thing, so much so that one day he can't stop, he just can't do it. Then they call and ask to see the books, and for a whole season he stands there before the others who look at the books and make their observations.

The child says there are men who don't stop, they never stop, standing there before her that's what he points out, and you don't know who those men are, whether they are indeed men or whether they mightn't be those wooden figures you see in fairgrounds, however closely you might look at them you still can't tell, that's what he says. That those men start up all over again, they can't help starting what they've been asked to do all over again. Words, phrases and everything that goes with them, the gestures, the looks and everything that follows on. To the point of exhaustion, great weariness and sleepless nights, yes it must be exhaustion, how could it not be exhaustion, he's been there a long time now, on the same path, the same interminable road on which he walks straight ahead each day putting his feet in the previous day's footsteps. That must be what he says to himself, there must come a point when the son tells himself that he's been there for a long time, when he feels exhaustion, boredom, terrible sadness. While he starts again, can't help starting again. And we know very well what that means, we know too well what it is to want nothing of what we do and say, and in the end we can no longer cope with the sadness, we shout in the night, all those black, black nights, those nights of fog and snow, and no one now, no, no one hears. We know it very well, and we wonder where habit stops, and that other thing begins, that thing that is so frightening, which clings to us as closely as our shadows, that's what we wonder. Yes, so where and how could we possibly know?

As he starts again, powerless not to, there before them it may be her voice that he hears, perhaps she is the one who has been speaking from the start as she spoke before, in the days before he even knew what a register was, when he had not yet arrived where her voice sent him, with those unchanging words, and the silences and the backs turned towards him, until in the end he heard nothing, knew nothing but the sound the words make, the words lost in the swirl of a river, a deafening roar, ever more powerfully the river flows and drags him away, he sees and hears it rolling its wild and powerful waters around, from the very start the river that has carried him off along with the animals and the dead wood and everything it has to carry off. When there is nothing there he sees it, he hears it, and then he tells himself that he has been there for a long time, that he, the son, has been there for a good long time, he feels the exhaustion and the cold that makes him shiver, there in the great, unbearable heat, the cold that is getting to him.

We saw the pale, transparent eyes gleaming in the half-light, gently, calmly like the dying fire, his eyes pale and shining, dilated beneath their wide grey lids. There before us, in his wet clothes, all his old woollens wrapped around him, although he didn't say much he told the story, we were sitting around her by the fire, we heard the wind starting up again, and the last sounds in the copse, and sometimes we would ask a question, about the books and the papers and the masters there were over there, and how long it had been, yes if the boy knew how long. In the shadow we saw that pallor gleam, that pearly pallor, the eyes he raised towards us now, looking at us now, one after the other and her last of all, he looked at her, he couldn't stop looking at her.

As to the story, he didn't need to say a thing and we still heard it, he could stay there with his back to the wall keeping his words to himself, murmuring and whispering as best he could, just replying with a yes or a no to the few questions we asked, he could stay that way on that night and others, until he became a stone or a log or one of those saplings that lined the lane he came up by. There was no need now for him to speak, no need for anything. Later, there was no need even to ask anyone to read the papers he gave her, which she stowed one after the other in her apron pocket. There before her in his clothes, dripping with snow, murmuring and whispering in that language he spoke and in which every now and again we could make out a phrase or the sound of a word, motionless as a statue, rough and grey as wood, as freshly carved stone, and everything hewn from the cold, winter and frost, murmuring and whispering what could only be murmured and whispered; unless sometimes you uttered a great cry, and then everyone heard and wondered why you were crying and what that cry could be.

What he had to say he said to her, better than anyone, and we in turn understood, we understood all about the men carried off by the rivers along with the animals and the dead wood. While she took the papers and stowed them in her apron, then with her gaunt hands she crossed and uncrossed her shawl over her chest, standing against the table, small and frail and more worn than a dry wooden twig, and you didn't even have to look at her to see her, eyes closed, in the blackest night anyone could have seen her and never forgotten her, taking and receiving the papers, the pages he showed her, all the pages, all the registers; and all the clearings he pointed to, and all the shacks that no one saw and where they settled one day, right close by, the son and others like him who didn't come and say anything, who didn't say they were coming back, and settled in a shack right close by, as close as they could be. The boy pointed to the desolation of the winter evening, of all winter evenings, telling her, coming to tell her that after looking for land as he had looked for it, then keeping his records in the registers, the son, the last of the boys, had come back, with the same momentum, the same endless urge to walk, he had come back and died in the depths of the copse, very close by in a shack that he had built himself.

It wasn't the little he said, it was the fact that watching him, the child, we understood, as we had never understood anything at all, about the ones carried off by the rivers and about things that had no end; and we understood that what we were watching and listening to, that grey winter evening, was nothing but time itself. There before us on those letters, those pages torn from the registers, it was time he was showing her, with a great gesture of his hand turned pale with the cold, the swollen hand that held out and brandished what it had to hold out and brandish. The time it had taken for it all to happen, and for the child to point, wordlessly, hand and arm outstretched, as though apart from watching over the dead and coming to find old women in their houses on snowy nights it was all he knew and all he had ever known, showing pages and words written on pages, and clearings and shacks in copses in the wood, and also the time it took for that to happen, all the time since the beginning. Yes that gesture towards her with which he told her what he had come to tell her, what she waited to be told, time and what they knew of it, the two of them a lifetime apart, and about the seas and the oceans and even more than that, the centuries, worlds unknown for ever, time and crazed rivers rolling their wild and violent waters, and all the days, months and years it took to get there, and then one day you said to yourself that it had all gone on long enough, you felt that great exhaustion, the cold that made you shiver, there in all the great heat the cold that finally got to you.

Eleven

He leaves. One last time he crosses the island. With the child and the dog following behind, he crosses the island, the plains, the great cane-fields, they go towards the sea they saw from up in the highlands. Towards the port where the ships are, the northern port, the southern port, they don't know. He is coming back, probably telling himself he's coming back, that he's done with the island now, he's leaving, having walked enough, kept enough records in the register, and doing what was asked of him in the correct fashion, yes, the correct fashion, the way you spend day after day keeping a promise, paying off a debt. One last time he crosses the cane-fields, the furnace of the plains, in the distance now he sees the hills, the *mornes* where it rains, where the coffee flowers bloom in April and from where you could see the sea down below, there were days when it shone in the sun, when it glittered with all its blue, yes without a doubt he talks about the sea that they saw from up there on days when the sky was clear.

Far as she sends him the son comes back, he repeats the voyage. And one evening when he is by the ships with the boy, having come back down the hills and crossed the plain to the sea, one evening they find themselves, the boy and the dog, among the departing ships. In the cove where they are standing they see the ship preparing to leave, and the men with the sacks and barrels in the scows. He said they could board that ship and go, he and the boy, that they would cross the sea, they would keep the books, they would do the accounts or whatever was required, throughout the crossing they would work like that to pay their crossing, yes, they would pay their crossing, that's what he says, and that it would be a kindness for them to be taken aboard that ship.

He is coming back, he writes that he is coming back, that he is crossing the sea and the oceans once again, he speaks of the contrary winds and the time it will take to get here, the point of that letter, one of the last, is to talk about that long, long voyage, longer even than the first and even harder, people on the ship have contracted fevers and men are being thrown overboard, they are being thrown into the waves in sacks along with the earth that the sailors put in the sacks, men are dying, they are suffering from all the illnesses that have existed since the sea has been the sea and the ships are nothing but stench, brackish water in their tubs and the cries of cattle, pregnant sows and chickens that have gone out of their minds. Yes the point of that letter, almost the last of them, is to talk about the terrible voyage and the sailors waiting for the wind, swearing on the most distant seas that they will never set sail again.

And when they both arrive they are seen here in the streets and the alleys and over by the warehouses. When they get here we don't know, but one day in early spring they are seen around here, at the very beginning of spring when the gorse comes into blossom, it must be spring, we remember the gorse blossoming and in puffs, in great, sweet waves the scent of whitethorn all over the hillside.

Yes however far she sends the son back he comes. But it isn't to come up and find her, to stand there before her after all that time, all those years they have spent apart. He doesn't come to find her as you might expect him to, and say the things you say after all that time, after so many years, that he's back and that he is still her most devoted and respectful son who has not forgotten her and who is there now standing before her, who has come with the express intention of greeting her and telling her his news. When he comes back that isn't what he does, he doesn't go to find her or take her in his arms, or even tell her of his return. When he comes back he looks for the clearing, up there on the hillside not even two leagues away from here, the quarter of an acre he needs for his shack, and up there he asks if there mightn't be a bit of copse, a scrap of land that no one was using.

And no one recognizes him or understands, no one says that it's him, Gertie's boy coming back after such a long absence and building we don't know why a shack in the copse, we don't know why after looking for land and keeping records as he did in the registers, now, the son, the last of them, further off and higher up in the copse, has a shack to build with a porch and columns. No one knows or says anything of the kind. Not about the son who has come back, who can do nothing but come back, nor about the shack that he sets about building.

Nor even about the passing of time. All the time so long awaited, the time it takes to grow so cold, for the cold grips him like a puddle in a rut, like a field mouse on the path, and then one snowy evening the boy goes up to see her, and he stands before her with all those papers he gives her one after the other, and he barely needs to speak, you'd think he has no more need to speak than she to hear. There before her with all those sheets which he holds out and which she stows one after the other in her apron, while over in the copse he points to the clearing that she can't see, that she has never seen, there in all the grey, the cold of winter and very close to her the clearing where the son is dying without her knowledge, that's what he comes to tell her, that the son, the last of the boys, is dying and so close to her, and that he will never, ever show his face again. Yes, all the time she has spent waiting like that, and in the end he settles there in the copse to die, never showing his face to her, or to anyone who knows her, that's what she understands, what there is to understand. Not only does he die – and the grief there is when sons die, and when they die very close by and you don't see them again – not only does he die, but he doesn't come and find her, his mother, or take her in his arms after all that time, all those years, after all that time he doesn't come up to see his mother, he doesn't tell her he has come back, the son, the last one, when he comes back all he does is look for a quarter of an acre and build his shack, and it's never finished, and everyone says that on the hillside close by there's this fellow who is never done building a shack, day after day he builds a shack, with wooden shingles, a porch and two light wood columns.

He settles there without a word in a corner of the copse and with the image of that shack in his mind, his sole idea now seems to be to build that shack around him, as though nothing else existed now or had never existed, as though before he built it, even before he had had the shadow of a notion of a shack in his head, it had been there in the clearing in the copse with its porch, its columns and its avenue of trees.

However far she sends him, back he comes, with that way he has of coming back, without saying a word or showing his face, he comes back the way you come back when you have accomplished your task, and he finds this bit of copse, this bit of waste land with its sweet grass, telling himself that he has found what he was looking for and that he's very nearly there, telling himself that and setting about building his shack, tile by tile. When he looks in this direction he sees the waste land as well as the roofs of our barns, the smoke above the rooftops, he looks at our barns and our roofs, and he tells himself that he's very close now, he's as close as he can be after this time, that's what he says and soon everyone understands, every one of us here, while evening falls and the snow won't let up, all around on the copse and on the river, the snow that is never done falling, after all that time he sees the roofs and the smoke above the rooftops, he hears the dogs in the farm-yards and he tells himself that they are the dogs from these parts, that's what he tells himself. That from where he is he can see the smoke from our chimneys and hear the dogs from these parts.

Settling up there in the clearing with all those things he has to say, day after day bringing up the planks and building the shack, and it takes longer than you could imagine, it takes the whole of summer and the following autumn, and he still doesn't say who he is, and nor does he come to find her, all that time that we see him with his planks and his wheelbarrow he doesn't come to find her, although it isn't because he doesn't want to, we know that, we can tell ourselves that, who's to say even whether in the evening he doesn't come prowling over here, prowling all around her as though she were a shadow, an unforgettable smell, sniffing like a dog the air she breathes, like a dog, the smell, the memory of days long gone, very close to the house where she lived, where she lives still. Where with her thighs open wide, and that's more years ago than we can count, she gave birth to him. Half an hour to get there and as long to get back, in the copse at nightfall who would see him? Yes in the evening before heading back towards the harbour, perhaps he comes prowling around her, around the hovel where she is making her soup, perhaps he comes to contemplate the smoke rising from the chimney, the thin, pungent smoke of peat and the chestnuts or apples she puts in the ashes, the smoke that says she's still there, that she always has been. Yes, isn't it he who sets our dogs off barking in the evening, all that autumn they've done nothing but bark?

And when there's none of that left to be done, carrying the planks, carving them and building what he has to build in the way of walls, porch and roof, he sets about making the bench for the porch, saying that under that porch what you need is a bench, to sit and watch the day drawing to a close and all there is to look at in the evening after work, he talks about the bench he needs, one day with three planks he makes the bench he talks about under the porch and he sits himself down, he looks to see if the bench is where it should be, and if from that bench you can see as you should be able to the avenue of trees and between the trees the grass he has sown and which is starting to come up, the lawns like the ones at the big houses, so green and so fine that you would be afraid of crushing them; he talks about the avenues you walk on, you walk on an avenue, the tender grass of an avenue, and right at the end in the gap of light, in the daylight between the trees, you catch sight of the porch and the columns of the porch, the house they come back to in the evening.

He makes the bench, he finishes the shack, that's what she understands, what we are busy telling her at the moment. One day he, the last of the boys, considers that he is finishing his job, he considers there is nothing more to do, nothing to undo of what he has done, and that everything is as it should be. He finishes the job and then he has to take the time to contemplate it, all he wants now, all he seems to want is a little time to contemplate his work, to sit down outside and look at the finished job, saying to himself what you say to yourself at such moments, saying he is happy it has all been possible, that there has been a time to build his dwelling and another to contemplate it, the light wooden porch and the trees leading up to it, the green, green avenue, and further off between the trees the patch of sky, beyond the avenue the sky you would need when you take a rest on the bench in the evening. He has that to tell himself, that's why we can see him sitting outside contemplating his work, telling himself that it's finished and it's a real dwelling with walls and a roof, and even a whole avenue of trees and tender grass at the end of which you can just see the porch and the columns of the dwelling. He walks as far as the shack, as far as the porch where the bench is, and then he turns round and sits down and he sees the sky between the trees, and right at the end the opposite shore with its fields and meadows, the church tower, the roofs of a village.

That's what he does. That's what she is told, what she hears. Behind her, behind the wall, we point to the forest, pointing to the shack that the son is building. After walking and keeping his records as she knows he does, one day the son builds the shack, he is never done building it, then he finishes it, he really has to finish it, such a small shack, he finishes it and once that's done he has some time, he has some time left, yes he has a little time left so that he can contemplate it, he contemplates it as much as he can. When he stops he contemplates the shack as he has never contemplated anything before, the shingle walls, the porch and the light wood columns and the avenue leading up to them. After finishing the shack he contemplates it he, the son, the last of the boys, has time to contemplate it.

And after that, no one knows. No one says to himself that he takes that time before settling down on his straw mattress. No one knows that moment, no one senses it, not even she. Before settling on the straw mattress, the bed of painted fabrics, the moment he takes to contemplate. To say that he has built a very fine and pleasant shack. He stops time, there is that moment of which she knows nothing and which we come to tell her about, when he, the son, stops time, the crazed river and its violent waters, that moment when everything stops around him. Torn from the world and time, unknown to anyone, that moment when the river, the great river, stops, or, before reaching the vast sea, before picking you up again the river slows down and sets you gently on the shore. The best, the sweetest of deaths, that moment without beginning or end when sometimes time stands still, and the world around you, and nothing exists either before or after, nothing exists of what is to come, not even that other death, the true, the great cold, dark death that rides its horses through the night and whistles in the December air, from the end of the world, that place he has known for ever, the greedy great mouth to which the rivers lead.

There in the shack in the copse one day, for one moment he, the returning son, the one who can do nothing but return, stops the river, stops all the rivers, all the violent waters, we see him stopping the river, stopping the voice that has spoken since the beginning. Before lying down on his straw mattress, his bed of painted fabrics, we see him stopping time and everything that can be stopped, and we have a glimpse of what he is thinking, yes, we think we know. We tell ourselves that if we had passed by we would have seen him on the bench looking at the avenue and the columns of the porch and all the sky there was between the trees, and we would have asked what he was doing on the bench at that time of day, or something else of the kind. But we never passed by or asked any questions, and they were alone on those days like the others, himself, the dog and the boy, and if the boy had any questions he said nothing, he didn't speak at all, no one said anything, they waited with the dog, they had to wait, as you wait for all those things you know without knowing them, those things you see coming in the end. Yes, they suspected that something was happening, they couldn't help suspecting as much.

And it doesn't necessarily take all that long, long enough, before lying down on his straw mattress, to contemplate the shack that he has built around him, not in fact very long at all, it only takes him a very short time. And autumn is already beginning, no rain yet, a fine light at evening on the hillside and further off towards the sea a fine, clear light, and the smells rising up from the bank, the waste land all around, the smells from the slope just before winter comes, when there is still warmth and mildness, we said that it was a lovely season, it wasn't raining yet, no it hadn't started raining yet, there was that great mildness in the air.

Twelve

And when he has finished, when he has spent long enough contemplating what he had to contemplate, he sends the boy to the other side of the river to find the fabrics he needs, discarded at the factory gates the fabrics they have no use for down there, red and blue, and all the birds the flowers and the spirals there are on them, he goes to get them and asks to be given them if it isn't too much trouble, it would be very kind, and when he returns with the fabrics painted with the loveliest designs in the loveliest colours, he is still there, the son, under the porch contemplating his work, saying that he has built a very fine, a very pleasant shack, and that it's a good thing it's finished, all the time he is stitching the fabric around the straw he talks about the shack which is as it should be, and of the exhaustion and the fevers that he feels coming, he says he feels the fevers coming, a very great exhaustion, that he has never suffered like that from fevers and exhaustion, he sews the fabric on the straw, the barrowful of dry leaves.

And then he settles in there and no one sees him again, none of us do, not around the harbour or on the hillside, only the boy passing by with his baskets now, every day since the rains began. He lies down on his straw mattress, his bed of painted fabrics, and he doesn't leave it again, he stays there without moving and no one knows, no one knows he is doing it or for how long he plans to stay like that, longer without a doubt than would leave him with a taste for going out and breathing the air of these parts like anyone else doing his share of work. Facing his wall in there he barely speaks, barely answers when the boy comes with soup and boiled meat, and when evening falls and the boy goes off again he, the son, has still not moved, he doesn't move, he stays with the dog and the bowls of soup and boiled meat cold as the copse, the hillside and the air around him; the bowls he barely touches, he takes neither soup nor boiled meat, and soon it is the dog that finishes what remains, next day when the boy comes the bowl on the ground is clean and shining, smooth as the finest china.

No he barely speaks, barely moves or turns when the boy comes, he stays there without moving or saying a word, seeing and hearing him talk to him, calling him gently, but staying there without moving or saying a word, so much so that the boy wonders if he need still speak, need still call gently to him, say his name as he touches his hand, his shoulder, as night falls, the rain, noisy and interminable, every afternoon on the roof and all around on the copse. He sees him and hears him leaning over him with his bowl and asking him to eat, and gently calling to him. The boy beside him talking and calling and wondering what he should do; he must see and hear him, and know too that he is looking at him, feeling and perhaps sensing that gaze upon him, a little higher up, by his shoulder, by the nape of his neck that place where people look at you when you turn your back, he turns his back, just turns away. Yes, the boy who comes and comes back day in day out, who calls him and leans over him, all the afternoons, all the evenings it takes, until nightfall and all that shadow up there in the wood, and in the shack you can't make out a thing now, neither of the son nor of the red and blue flowers, nor of the bowls on the ground, the boy, he must hear him, he must know he is there, talking to him, looking at him. Unless, once again, she is the one who comes and goes around him just as she did before, and she who utters all her words, all those things she has been saying since the very beginning, unless it is she buzzing around him with all her words like an insect in the house, and that is all you can hear, she is all you can hear, one season after another and also during the winter when everything rests. And in the morning it is the cold that wakes you, the cold that gets into the body and won't leave it, the bones the muscles steeped in the damp cold of the earth, of the wood around him, the white light rising from the ground, brushing against the beaten earth, slowly rising up along the tiles of the wall, he smells the scent of earth and dead leaves, and another smell that has come from far away, bitter and almost sweet.

He doesn't come and see her or say those things you say after such a long time, after all those years, that's what she understands, that the son, the last one, has settled in the shack in the copse and doesn't show his face to her, he stays there without moving or saying a word. He stays on his bedding for as long as it takes and the boy comes to bring him soup and boiled meat that he doesn't touch, it's the dog that laps the bowls, that's how time passes, the last months, the last days, and now there are evenings when he weeps, it's quite possible that now in the evening the son begins to weep, when evening falls it may well be that he weeps and the boy sees his shoulders heaving, hears some sort of noise, a muffled groan, so he weeps along with him as evening falls, evening falls and they weep together in the shack, so much so that in her turn she sees him, without a doubt she sees the son weeping as he used to, slowly, with great hoarse noises, something breaking away in his throat, the faint sound of something tearing.

He is waiting, we tell her. He goes on waiting. As long as it takes. The end of autumn, and December through to Christmas. Not dying straight away. Waiting for winter to come, as harsh and windy as the previous one, waiting for the cold to seize hold of him all of a sudden like pond water, like a puddle in a road. Pinning him to his pallet without further ado; leaving him nothing more to ask, nothing more to wait for, and then the dog starts howling as much as a dog can howl, and you can hear it everywhere, at the port and at the drydock and on the other side as far as the farms, the dog, and the boy in his turn shouting, running all across the hillside, so that we climb up there by the copse and the tree-felling area, and when we get there we find him there, the son, rolled up as though asleep, wrapped in the same rags as the ones lashed around his bedding, the barrowful of straw and dry leaves, and near him the boy watching over him without moving or saying anything as though it were all he had ever done, watching over the departed and staying there without moving or saying a word, not even looking at you when you talk to him, looking at the wall in front of him and everything that is behind the wall, the little wood on the cliffs and, further off, the sea they came by, in spite of the snow, in spite of the grey; perhaps he sees the sea and everything there is over there in the way of islands and coffee plantations, except that the cold is coming, the rain from inland, the one as motionless as the other on the ground where the shavings still lie, fair and grey as the hair at his nape, at his nape we see the grey curls, escaping from all the wool and the cloths the curls of hair, tired, grey, gentle and lifeless in the grey evening.

Then for the sake of looking at him we look at him. But time must have passed. We don't really recognize him. Even that evening we can't really recognize him. The son, old Gertie's last boy, is one thing, another the man on his straw mattress, lying curled up as though asleep, we can't even straighten him, by the time we get there he's too cold, too stiff, like a branch. We say that with such cold weather it was bound to happen, and it's the cold and all this winter we're having, and it's unfortunate, yes, it's unfortunate, we say all those things that you think and say at such times, then we take off our hats and pray, and all the time we are praying we look at him, we look at his shoulders and the nape of his neck, everything that peeps out from between the rags, and one of us says he has a look of Gertie's son, talking about the curls over his forehead and his face, the gentleness in his face, around his lips, around his broad temples, then we ask the boy what the man's name is and if he's from around here, but he doesn't reply, he doesn't look as though he wants to reply, and we stop thinking about it. We have to believe that we're mistaken. That's what we say. That we are mistaken and that it isn't Gertie's son, the last of the boys, it can't be him, seeing as how she's still getting letters from over there, yes, she's still getting letters. In order to stop thinking about it, we forget again. It must be the case that we have to forget, that's what it must be. In our opinion we've got to forget.

We forget that it's the returning son, we forget who it is in the clearing in the copse, we forget the clearing and all the time he's been lying on his straw mattress, we look at him and we forget him, lying as if he had always been on the bed of straw and painted fabrics, with the cords that scratch his skin, marking it vivid pink, and sometimes an insect runs all about the place, in all directions on the cold earth floor, the jumble of straw and beaten earth, throughout the whole of the winter, in all the darkness here a stag-beetle, a weevil.

We forget and we forget, but looking at him with this shack around him, we say that what he's made is not a dwelling. That in our opinion, all the time we've seen him coming and going with his planks and his wheelbarrow, what he had in mind was something other than a dwelling. Something other than a place to live and collect your energy in the evening for tomorrow's tasks. No, it couldn't have been a dwelling that he had in mind, that he saw fit to call a dwelling, that's what we say, that's what we realize. Just as she has no need to see or hear anything, except the shack in the clearing, and the little daylight there is, the grey, grey cold, while the son is there on his jumble of cloths that will end up scratching his skin, all curled up, all askew and his knees as folded as knees can be, he looks like a child there on his jumble of straw and beaten earth, and not far away, all through the shack in one direction then another, the insect that has escaped the winter, all around him the insect coming and going, the insect that has survived the cold and the snow and everything that would normally finish those insects off.

No it's not worth talking about, not worth asking questions about, no one talks or asks any questions, there are things we've known since the very beginning, things we've known for ever. We think about the blue sky and the mildness there sometimes is in the air, in the spring and in the summer. We think about it as we have never thought about it before. We think about it as though we were thinking about something we would like to see again and will not see again, yes, grief must cross our paths; we say that we will never again see anything of the things we love, the spring and the hoof-beats of the horses in the meadow, or the sky in the water of the pools, blue, mauve, and immediately afterwards a fringe of fog, the pink of a big cloud, or the sweet, warm rain like the wind from the sea. Up where the river bends when we feel the sea wind coming, the wind that blows the ships from America to here.

When he goes. When all we see is his back, the woollens he's wrapped up in, on the lane when he passes the ponds, at the bottom of the sky the little silhouette moving away with the same even step, reaching the copse, the bottom of the hillside, as though it were all he had ever done, coming to find old women in their houses then going back the way he had come, and yet it won't stop snowing, on the forest and further off on the river. The snow won't stop, any more than he will stop standing there in front of her, pale eyes wide, a pale and shining gaze beneath his broad grey lids, pointing to the copse in the wood, pointing to the wild and raging rivers, pointing to the beginning and the end of the story, vast and unforgettable, in the shadow we see that pallor gleam, that pearly pallor, the eyes of the boy who won't stop standing against the door, telling what he knows.

Everything against us; all that remains the cold and the deep, heavy night, and sometimes the cry of an animal in the copse, you'd wonder if there had ever been anything else, if even for one day around here there had been anything but the cold and the deep, heavy night, it won't stop snowing, and nor will he stop going off by the sunken lane, turning his back and going and when she does begin to move it's to come to the window and look out towards the farms to see if she can still make him out.

She doesn't need anyone to come and find her by the snowy paths with bundles of sheets and pages, or to be told of a shack with a porch and columns that a son of hers is building close by. Nor even that it is the snow or the rain or the sun rising and setting. She only needs to see him a little longer, that boy turning away from her, greyer and greyer, smaller and smaller over by the ponds, soon impossible to make out at the bottom of the sky, in the grey of winter.

And when she turns towards us it is to say that it would be kind of us to read her what is written there on the papers, then we go and get the schoolboy from les Vignelles and he reads what there was to read, he reads until late in the night, and when the candle goes out she goes and gets another one, she says sorry for the trouble of making him read all that, the letters that were never sent, never put in the sacks on the ships and the ones written on the pages of the books, the ones he started, and then everything gets mixed up, letters and records, he reads until late in the night, while one after another she takes the sheets and the pages and she puts them back in her apron pocket, and when he has finished she goes back to the firewood, resting all her weight on her cane she sits down in the corner by the firewood and wishes us goodnight, she says she is going to take a little rest, and the following day at the same time we drop by again and she is still there clutching her parcel of pages, she is there with all her pages looking at us, for the sake of looking at us she looks at us, but this time it isn't either to say hello or goodnight, or any of the things she has been saying over the past twenty years when she sees us coming.

And we stay there in silence. Andrès, Ange Berthomé and Petit-Jean from les Vignelles. In all that cold, in all the depth of that night. We think about the rivers and the time it takes to go down the rivers to get to the deep sea after which there is nothing. We think about the stories told by the men from the ships, the sailors who cross the seven seas and the others who bring down the wood, down from the mountains, we think about the stories we are afraid to hear, and we go down, we say we have to go down now and talk about what we know, that's what we say, that we have to tell that story. We go down to find the men from the ships, but soon we don't know who we have come to talk about, old Gertie or that last son, or maybe the boy from America. It's as though we no longer know what we know, we don't know about the beginning or the end of the story, or even whether it all has a beginning and an end. We are there in all the cold, all the winter all around, and sometimes one of us turns round, saying you never know when stories like that one are going to happen. That there are things like that which you don't really know, can't know.

And by the time we've reached the quarries we can make out the first fires, the inns and the lights of the town. We go and find the men from the ships and say we've come to talk about the son of the old woman from les Lutz, the last one, who is dead in the shack, he was the one who brought all his planks down to the port with the child and the dog, Gertie's son, the last one he was, we say that, that much we can say. As to the rest, as to men who don't stop doing what they're doing, and the rivers that carry them off with everything there is to carry off in the way of trees, men and animals, we say nothing about that, yes, there must be things you don't say, things you will never say, we don't say the rest.

We remember him, pacing up and down the hillside with his planks and keeping his records in the books. He walks, he keeps his records in his books, then he walks again, he comes down the hills, he paces up and down the hillsides with his planks, he walks, we see him walking on a hillside, a slope, quickening his pace, slipping between sacks and riggings, the big red and brown sails of the returning ships, walking under the rain, and sometimes he turns round, he looks at the river and the fishermen's houses, the mills and the roofs on the opposite shore where the sun appears from time to time, illuminating a field of grass, a vine, he looks at the grass shining in the sun, the pale earth of the vines, soon all he can see is the grey sky and the rain clouds and ahead of him where he is going, the copse in the forest and the clearing where the shack is, he contemplates the shack then he lies down, he stays there without moving or saying a word as though he were asleep, we see him, we look at the man who has just died in front of us, who has not disappeared, has not vanished into oblivion, the sweltering heat of a savannah, we see him dead in front of us and that boy beside him, and then we say that nothing comes to an end.

As soon as winter comes we tell the story, there's always one of us there to tell it, Andrès, Ange Berthomé and Petit-Jean from les Vignelles, all of us who found him in the shack and the boy at his side. They must be inside us, those cries that we dare not utter. We don't dare slash the black night with those cries we hear within us. Yes, it must be winter, and inside us those cries that no one hears, that no one knows, those cries we utter on winter evenings, on evenings when the rain comes down.

Some years more than others we wait for spring. We wait for the blue sky and the mildness of the wind, the river down below, blue as the sea, and the sun on the sails of the ships. No one crosses the hillside up there any more. The yews have grown and you can see them in the distance now, you need only climb up to the gardens, up to that place they call Miseri, from a distance you can see the dark line, the double ridge leading up to the porch, to the two pale wooden columns. That winter we went to fetch him, up behind the ash trees and we brought him back to the shack, we said to ourselves that was how it had to be.

In the port at evening we can make out the boy with the dog, they watch the ships arriving and the ships setting off, the wind rises up driving the clouds across the river and further inland, the sun returns, gently colouring the sails drying on the stone. At nightfall they make their way back to the old parts of town, in the sky the greys and the blues gradually yield to black, to shades of dark purple and, above them when the rain stops, a quick pale cloud, carried on the wind.